2012

Guideposts

DAILY PLANNER

Seeing God's Handiwork Every Day

All the days ordained for me were written in your book.

—PSALM 139:16 (NIV)

Guideposts
New York, New York

Guideposts Daily Planner 2012

ISBN-10: 0-8249-6494-2
ISBN-13: 978-0-8249-6494-8

Published by Guideposts
16 East 34th Street
New York, New York 10016
Guideposts.org

Distributed by Ideals Publications, a Guideposts company
2630 Elm Hill Pike, Suite 100
Nashville, Tennessee 37214

ACKNOWLEDGMENTS

Every attempt has been made to credit the sources of copyrighted material used in this book. If any such acknowledgment has been inadvertently omitted or miscredited, receipt of such information would be appreciated.

All Scripture quotations, unless otherwise noted, are taken from *The Holy Bible, New King James Version*. Copyright © 1997, 1990, 1985, 1983 by Thomas Nelson, Inc.

Scripture quotations marked (KJV) are taken from *The King James Version of the Bible*.

Scripture quotations marked (NEB) are taken from *The New English Bible*. Copyright © The Delegates of the Oxford University Press and the Syndics of the Cambridge University Press 1961, 1970.

Scripture quotations marked (NIV) are taken from *The Holy Bible, New International Version*. Copyright © 1973, 1978, 1984 International Bible Society. Used by permission of Zondervan Bible Publishers.

Scripture quotations marked (NLT) are taken from the *Holy Bible*, New Living Translation. Copyright © 1996. Used by permission of Tyndale House Publishers, Inc., Wheaton, Illinois 60189. All rights reserved.

Edited by Lucile Allen
Cover and interior design and typesetting by Müllerhaus
Cover photo by Getty Images
Interior photos by iStock

Printed and bound in the United States of America
10 9 8 7 6 5 4 3 2 1

Guideposts

DAILY PLANNER 2012

All the days ordained for me were written in your book.

—PSALM 139:16 (NIV)

Between the
Last of '11 and
The first of '12,
Midnight sounds:
Pealing church bells
Ring out the old,
Ring in the new—
A resonant reminder of
What I myself should do.
Father,
Your great Apostle Paul
Told the church at Ephesus,
"Put on the new man,"
Urging the people there
To cast out old habits
Not Christ-taught.
Let me follow that
Good advice tonight
And start this new year
As Your child of light.

Jesus realized the merits of childhood and charged His followers to become like little children. Wouldn't that be wonderful if we could once again possess those characterics? If we could maintain our maturity and yet experience the simplicity and excitement of a child? What a difference it would make in our lives—and our faith! We would have more energy to deal with our problems. We would find more joy in relationships. We would see fresh opportunities and solutions.

Wouldn't this year of 2012 be a good time to embark on the adventure of becoming as a child again? Are you ready for a fresh year of joy and laughter, of wonder and discovery? Are you ready to be surprised by what new life and vitality is in store for you if you practice a childlike faith? We can break that task down and work on one quality each month.

—Mary Lou Carney

JANUARY 2012

SUNDAY	MONDAY	TUESDAY	WEDNESDAY	THURSDAY	FRIDAY	SATURDAY
1	2	3	4	5	6	7
8	9	10	11	12	13	14
15	16	17	18	19	20	21
22	23	24	25	26	27	28
29	30	31				

Notes

DECEMBER

S	M	T	W	T	F	S
				1	2	3
4	5	6	7	8	9	10
11	12	13	14	15	16	17
18	19	20	21	22	23	24
25	26	27	28	29	30	31

FEBRUARY

S	M	T	W	T	F	S
			1	2	3	4
5	6	7	8	9	10	11
12	13	14	15	16	17	18
19	20	21	22	23	24	25
26	27	28	29			

"Dad, come quick! Listen to this!" I heard Andy's voice calling me. He had been playing the piano for half an hour. I couldn't make out the tunes, although the note of triumph in his voice came through loud and clear. Now eleven, he had been tackling the instrument for nearly three years and had graduated from "Twinkle, Twinkle Little Star" to Beethoven's "Fur Elise," and other classical pieces. I strode into the living room, pride swelling in my chest.

The first thing I saw was a pair of feet hovering in midair. Andy was lying on the piano bench, flat on his stomach, his legs thrust out behind him and his face inches away from the keyboard.

"Look, Dad. I can play the piano with my nose!"

And so he could. I watched, astonished, as he picked out "Twinkle, Twinkle Little Star."

I didn't know what to say. This is why we spend all this money? Then Andy looked up at me with a sweet, goofy grin, and all the love in the world rushed into my heart. I began to laugh, and Andy laughed with me.

—Philip Zaleski

Prayer Requests Baby Emme, Megan + Josh, my Jim, Chris, Megan + SEAN health questions –

Need wisdom in Talking w/ my Kids.

Answered Prayers
SEAN CALLED
CHRIS IS A JOY IN THE HOUSE

God's Touch THE written word + discussion at bible st; Spirit's guidance when talking to Chris.

Grateful: Jim → he is listening + supportative. NICE WEATHER, no Snow.
A CABIN RETREAT, UNREAL!!!

Mom

1 SUNDAY

There is a time for everything…a time to weep and a time to laugh. —Ecclesiastes 3:1, 4 (NIV)
NEW YEAR'S DAY

GOOD NEIGHBORS
RECOUP DAY, TIRED AFTER MORANS.

Trish 7am

2 MONDAY

He will yet fill your mouth with laughing, and your lips with rejoicing. —Job 8:21

Jim off work. Afternoon errands.

3 TUESDAY

Sorrow is better than laughter, for sadness has a refining influence on us. —Ecclesiastes 7:3 (NLT)   _Mom_

Bible Study. Ex 12
(Nap AFTERNOON)

4 WEDNESDAY

Blessed are you who weep now, for you shall laugh. —Luke 6:21   _Talked to Sue_

Sleep Study 8:30 pm.
Grateful for Jims support. Hard discussion w/ CHRIS

5 THURSDAY

And Sarah said, "God has made me laugh, and all who hear will laugh with me." —Genesis 21:6

SLEPT GREAT?
Massage w/ Minda 2:30

CLEANED

6 FRIDAY

You will laugh at destruction and famine; wild animals will not terrify you. —Job 5:22 (NLT)

Chris apologized for hard discussion.
"HUNT + GATHER" errands
TO THE CABIN TONIGHT!

7 SATURDAY

She is clothed with strength and dignity, and she laughs without fear of the future. —Proverbs 31:25 (NLT)

CABIN — put up bunks
         worked on drapes

Caroline's mom, Franny passed away.

M om, you have to believe God!" my daughter Kendall told me emphatically one evening.

The results from a biopsy showed my ovarian cancer had spread to my lungs, confirming my Stage 4 status. I felt discouraged, and the lies had started seeping into my soul: *Cancer always wins. God doesn't hear your prayers.*

I knew these were lies from the enemy of my faith. But they grew bigger than God's promises as I allowed them to echo through my mind.

A few days later, Kendall walked in and plunked a wrapped package down on the kitchen counter. "To help you remember to believe God," she said.

Inside was a wooden block with letters spelling out BELIEVE.

I placed it on a windowsill above the sink and was stunned to see, for the first time, that the word LIE is tucked right there in the middle of the word BE-LIE-VE.

What a powerful reminder that I can focus on the LIE…or step back and BELIEVE God's truth, which is so much bigger: the truth that God knows our suffering and walks with us and will meet all our needs.

—Carol Kuykendall

Prayer Requests _____
_____
_____
_____

Answered Prayers _____
_____
_____
_____

God's Touch _____
_____
_____
_____

8
SUNDAY

Jesus said to him, "If you can believe, all things are possible to him who believes." —Mark 9:23

Call Caroline, Gloria for Joseph's Coat

9
MONDAY

"Look among the nations and watch—be utterly astounded! For I will work a work in your days which you would not believe, though it were told you." —Habakkuk 1:5

Joseph's Coat

10
TUESDAY

How then shall they call on Him in whom they have not believed? And how shall they believe in Him of whom they have not heard? —Romans 10:14

Bible Study

CHRIS TO CA 6AM.

11
WEDNESDAY

Immediately the father of the child cried out and said with tears, "Lord, I believe; help my unbelief!" —Mark 9:24

Joseph's Coat

12
THURSDAY

This is His commandment: that we should believe on the name of His Son Jesus Christ and love one another, as He gave us commandment. —1 John 3:23

13
FRIDAY

He who comes to God must believe that He is, and that He is a rewarder of those who diligently seek Him. —Hebrews 11:6

14
SATURDAY

Teach me good judgment and knowledge, for I believe Your commandments. —Psalm 119:66

I just read about the options that will be available on cars of the future, and I'm fighting back yawns. Why don't carmakers give us something we really need? I don't want windshield wipers that sense moisture and turn themselves on. I can tell when it's raining.

I'd like to see things like:

A heater that I could leave on low while I shop, so I could return to warm seats and clear windshields.

A horn for the rear bumper, so I could beep at the children playing behind me in the driveway or warn the tailgater to back off.

A foot-operated dimmer switch, so I don't have to take my hand off the wheel to dim the lights.

What applies to car makers applies to me, of course. Before buying that expensive gold watch for my wife, maybe I should ask her what she really wants. Maybe she'd rather have a new sewing machine.

How nice that we have a Father in heaven who urges us to tell Him our needs and wants, even though He already knows what they are.

—Daniel Schantz

Prayer Requests _____

_____

_____

_____

Answered Prayers _____

_____

_____

_____

God's Touch _____

_____

_____

_____

He knows the secrets of the heart. —Psalm 44:21

15
SUNDAY

The Lord is good, a stronghold in the day of trouble; and He knows those who trust in Him. —Nahum 1:7
MARTIN LUTHER KING JR. DAY

16
MONDAY

He reveals deep and secret things; He knows what is in the darkness, and light dwells with Him. —Daniel 2:22

17
TUESDAY

"The Lord knows those who are his." —2 Timothy 2:19

Dr. Gromer

18
WEDNESDAY

The Lord knows the days of the upright, and their inheritance shall be forever. —Psalm 37:18

19
THURSDAY

He knows the way that I take; when He has tested me, I shall come forth as gold. —Job 23:10

20
FRIDAY

For if our heart condemns us, God is greater than our heart, and knows all things. —1 John 3:20

21
SATURDAY

I remember going to my husband Norman's office whenever he needed to talk through something. "Lord," he'd say, "we have this problem. Please guide us in the right direction. Make us receptive to Your will. We thank You for Your help."

Then we'd sit quietly for a while. We never concentrated on the specific problem or on possible solutions. Instead, we tried to make our minds quiet and open. Sometimes, I'd think of some appropriate phrase from the Bible, like "In returning and rest you shall be saved; in quietness and confidence shall be your strength" (Isaiah 30:15) and focus on that. After a while, one of us would say to the other, "It seems to me this is the way to deal with this." Or, "I believe we've been on the wrong track with this one." It was uncanny how often the same conviction came to both of us and how often a clear line of action would open up.

If you're facing a problem or a decision, why not ask a friend or loved one to be your partner in prayer?

—Ruth Stafford Peale

Prayer Requests

_____
_____
_____
_____

Answered Prayers

_____
_____
_____
_____

God's Touch

_____
_____
_____
_____

Now My eyes will be open and My ears attentive to prayer made in this place. —2 Chronicles 7:15

22
SUNDAY

"When my soul fainted within me, I remembered the Lord; and my prayer went up to You, into Your holy temple." —Jonah 2:7

23
MONDAY

The effective, fervent prayer of a righteous man avails much. —James 5:16

24
TUESDAY

"We will give ourselves continually to prayer and to the ministry of the word." —Acts 6:4

25
WEDNESDAY

Let my prayer come before You; incline Your ear to my cry. —Psalm 88:2

26
THURSDAY

The Lord is far from the wicked, but He hears the prayer of the righteous. —Proverbs 15:29

27
FRIDAY

Be anxious for nothing, but in everything by prayer and supplication, with thanksgiving, let your requests be made known to God. —Philippians 4:6

28
SATURDAY

The Lord is my light and my salvation; whom shall I fear?
The Lord is the strength of my life; of whom shall I be afraid? —PSALM 27:1

I called home on a Sunday afternoon, when my parents are generally enjoying the peace and quiet of the day and the ample sections of the newspaper. I wanted to catch up a bit and see how the weekend had gone. My dad answered and proudly told me that Alex, my nephew, had learned his first Bible verse in Sunday school.

I scolded my dad for being one of those proud grandpas who believe that his twenty-one-month-old grandchild could be capable of memorizing, retaining and reciting anything more complicated than asking for a cookie. Dad laughed and said, "Just listen."

I heard him pass the phone to Alex and pick up on an extension.

"Alex," he said, "'Be not—'"

And very loudly from across the room, I heard this little voice pipe up. "'*Fwaid*," he said in his singsong tone.

I burst into laughter. *Be not afraid.* What a wonderful first lesson: to trust a loving and caring God. What a great reminder to a jaded aunt who needed to remember that through God, all things are possible, even a toddler's memory verse.

—Ashley Kappel

Prayer Requests _____

_____

_____

_____

Answered Prayers _____

_____

_____

_____

God's Touch _____

_____

_____

_____

29
SUNDAY

"Be strong and of good courage; do not be afraid, nor be dismayed, for the Lord your God is with you wherever you go." —Joshua 1:9

30
MONDAY

Now the Lord spoke to Paul in the night by a vision, "Do not be afraid, but speak, and do not keep silent." —Acts 18:9

31
TUESDAY

But immediately Jesus spoke to them, saying, "Be of good cheer! It is I; do not be afraid." —Matthew 14:27

FEBRUARY
1
WEDNESDAY

Then the angel said to them, "Do not be afraid, for behold, I bring you good tidings of great joy which will be to all people." —Luke 2:10

2
THURSDAY

In God I have put my trust; I will not be afraid. What can man do to me? —Psalm 56:11

3
FRIDAY

When I saw Him, I fell at His feet as dead. But He laid His right hand on me, saying to me, "Do not be afraid; I am the First and the Last." —Revelation 1:17

4
SATURDAY

Moses said to the people, "Do not be afraid. Stand still, and see the salvation of the Lord, which He will accomplish for you today." —Exodus 14:13

Sometimes, Father,
Frigid winter
Blankets my spirit.
Gray days become
A harsh and heavy burden.
And then I remember how
You promised Noah
Winter and summer,
Seedtime and harvest,
Day and night,
Cold and heat,
As long as the earth
shall live.
Help me to understand;
The barren and difficult times
Are not a curse,
But part of a blessing —
Your wonderful,
Everchanging gift:
Life.

IMAGINATION

As a child, one of my jobs was to carry drinking water to farmhands, but I was terrified of the huge Holsteins near the creek's edge. Then one Sunday, we sang, "It's just like Jesus to drive the cows away." That's what I thought the hymn said. From then on, whenever I was sent across the fields I pictured Jesus going with me. I sang and resang that chorus, watching the herd scatter before me. And I knew the true power of faith. (Years later I laughed to realize the word was clouds, not cows!)

This month, I'm going to dust off my imagination. I'm going to use it whenever I read the Bible—to feel the spray of the Jordan River, taste the unleavened bread broken at the table. I'm going to see with the eye of belief. Let's visualize God at work in our world: settling border disputes, clearing jams on freeway ramps, comforting weary travelers, touching sore muscles. This month, I choose to believe in the limitless possibilities of faith.

—Mary Lou Carney

FEBRUARY 2012

SUNDAY	MONDAY	TUESDAY	WEDNESDAY	THURSDAY	FRIDAY	SATURDAY
			1	2	3	4
5	6	7	8	9	10	11
12	13	14	15	16	17	18
19	20	21	22	23	24	25
26	27	28	29			

Notes

JANUARY

S	M	T	W	T	F	S
1	2	3	4	5	6	7
8	9	10	11	12	13	14
15	16	17	18	19	20	21
22	23	24	25	26	27	28
29	30	31				

MARCH

S	M	T	W	T	F	S
				1	2	3
4	5	6	7	8	9	10
11	12	13	14	15	16	17
18	19	20	21	22	23	24
25	26	27	28	29	30	31

Whatever the Lord pleases He does, in heaven and in earth,
in the seas and in all deep places. —PSALM 13:5

When I'm scheduled for a check-up or biopsy, I pray, "Please, Lord!" If I'm working on something important, I write, "Please, Lord!" in the margin of the paper. I think of it as a way of continually praying, "Please, Lord let this happen for me." Until recently, I never thought of it as selfish.

Then I met Maryann. She's a ninety-four-year-old convalescent-home resident who still speaks with the Irish brogue she brought to America as a sixteen-year-old girl. She has a fierce faith and is given to her own muttered prayers. When she's upset about anything she exclaims, "God bless us and save us!" When something goes well she says, "Thanks be to the Man above!"

At the end of every visit, I tell Maryann when I'll be back, and she always says a fervent "Please God!" At first, I thought that she was making this small prayer in the same spirit I made mine. But my prayer amounts to "Please, Lord, please me." Her prayer is "Lord, I hope this pleases You."

You can learn a lot from a ninety-four-year-old if you really listen.

—Marci Alborghetti

Prayer Requests _____

_____

_____

_____

_____

Answered Prayers _____

_____

_____

_____

_____

God's Touch _____

_____

_____

_____

_____

5
SUNDAY

When a man's ways please the Lord, He makes even his enemies to be at peace with him. —Proverbs 16:7

6
MONDAY

Then a voice came from heaven, "You are My beloved Son, in whom I am well pleased." —Mark 1:11

7
TUESDAY

So shall My word be that goes forth from My mouth; it shall not return to Me void, but it shall accomplish what I please. —Isaiah 55:11

8
WEDNESDAY

Be pleased, O Lord, to deliver me; O Lord, make haste to help me! —Psalm 40:13

9
THURSDAY

So then, those who are in the flesh cannot please God. —Romans 8:8

10
FRIDAY

"He who sent Me is with Me. The Father has not left Me alone, for I always do those things that please Him." —John 8:29

11
SATURDAY

But now God has set the members, each one of them, in the body just as He pleased. —1 Corinthians 12:18

*He who loves his brother abides in the light,
and there is no cause for stumbling in him.* —1 JOHN 2:10

Oh, bother! I thought, *I forgot to get cards!* It was late in the evening of February 13, and I had no Valentine cards to place on the breakfast table the next morning. Fortunately, I have a hoard of greeting cards sent to and received from various members of our family, all carefully saved in cardboard boxes.

Brilliant, I decided, *I'll just dig out some old cards and recycle love!*

I was up into the night, sorting Valentine's Day out from Christmas, Easter, birthdays and anniversary greetings. There were hand-drawn cartoons from our son, with stick figures and letters printed backward. The largest card was from my husband. It had silk roses surrounding a white lace heart with the words, "I always dreamed I'd find you."

Selecting dozens of cards, I put them all over the house—on the piano, in the bookcases, in the bathroom, the kitchen, and some in surprise places like closets and in the glove compartment of our car.

We spent days mulling over and giggling our way back through all the remember-whens of my recycled love. Forgotten cards? Nope. These were the best ever!

—Fay Angus

Prayer Requests _____
_____
_____
_____

Answered Prayers _____
_____
_____
_____

God's Touch _____
_____
_____
_____

12
SUNDAY

He who loves his life will lose it, and he who hates his life in this world will keep it for eternal life. —John 12:25
ABRAHAM LINCOLN'S BIRTHDAY

13
MONDAY

So husbands ought to love their own wives as their own bodies; he who loves his wife loves himself.
—Ephesians 5:28

14
TUESDAY

Beloved, let us love one another, for love is of God; and everyone who loves is born of God and knows God.
—1 John 4:7
VALENTINE'S DAY

TREATS FOR Bible Study

15
WEDNESDAY

He who gets wisdom loves his own soul; He who keeps understanding will find good. —Proverbs 19:8

16
THURSDAY

For the Father Himself loves you, because you have loved Me, and have believed that I came forth from God.
—John 16:27

17
FRIDAY

The Lord opens the eyes of the blind; the Lord raises those who are bowed down; the Lord loves the righteous.
—Psalm 146:8

18
SATURDAY

He who loves silver will not be satisfied with silver; nor he who loves abundance, with increase.
—Ecclesiastes 5:10

Now when he was in affliction, he implored the Lord his God, and humbled himself greatly before the God of his fathers. —2 CHRONICLES 33:12

Abraham Lincoln and I have a lot in common. He grew up in Indiana; I grew up in Indiana. He loved his mother very much; I loved my mother very much. He worked as a store clerk; I worked as a store clerk. He had a cat named Bob and a turkey named Jack; I had a dog named Ginger. He was president of the United States; I was…well, president of my senior class. Okay, maybe we aren't so very much alike. But I'd like to think that we share one important characteristic: Lincoln was a man of prayer. He prayed alone; he prayed for guidance; he prayed in gratitude. I try to begin every day this very same way.

"I have been driven many times upon my knees by the overwhelming conviction that I had nowhere else to go," said Lincoln. "My own wisdom and that of all about me seemed insufficient for that day."

This gives me one more way I can try to be like Lincoln: to be humble.

—Mary Lou Carney

Prayer Requests

Answered Prayers

God's Touch

19 SUNDAY	For whoever exalts himself will be humbled, and he who humbles himself will be exalted." —Luke 14:11
20 MONDAY	The humble He guides in justice, and the humble He teaches His way. —Psalm 25:9 PRESIDENTS' DAY
21 TUESDAY	Being found in appearance as a man, He humbled Himself and became obedient to the point of death, even the death of the cross. —Philippians 2:8
22 WEDNESDAY	Do not set your mind on high things, but associate with the humble. Do not be wise in your own opinion. —Romans 12:16 ASH WEDNESDAY / GEORGE WASHINGTON'S BIRTHDAY
23 THURSDAY	For the Lord takes pleasure in His people; He will beautify the humble with salvation. —Psalm 149:4
24 FRIDAY	Humble yourselves in the sight of the Lord, and He will lift you up. —James 4:10
25 SATURDAY	When pride comes, then comes shame; but with the humble is wisdom. —Proverbs 11:2

Patricia, a member of our church, announced one Sunday that she had shingles and asked for prayers. I dutifully prayed and extended my sympathy when she said she was having a lot of pain.

But it wasn't until I got shingles myself that I understood the pain she'd been talking about. My shingles had advanced enough before I discovered them that our doctor wasn't sure we could get them stopped. But strong doses of an antiviral medication, plus the prayers of our church members, including Patricia, set me on the road to recovery.

When Patricia said to me during the worst of it, "I know what you're going through," I knew she did, and that was a comfort. When other members of our church who had never experienced shingles touched my hand and said, "I'm sorry," that was a comfort too. But the greatest comfort of all came from the Friend above, Who listened to my prayers and held my hand at night when I couldn't sleep.

—Madge Harrah

Prayer Requests

_____
_____
_____
_____
_____

Answered Prayers

_____
_____
_____
_____
_____

God's Touch

_____
_____
_____
_____
_____

26
SUNDAY

In the multitude of my anxieties within me, Your comforts delight my soul. —Psalm 94:19

27
MONDAY

For whatever things were written before were written for our learning, that we through the patience and comfort of the Scriptures might have hope. —Romans 15:4

28
TUESDAY

"Therefore, behold, I will allure her, will bring her into the wilderness, and speak comfort to her." —Hosea 2:14

29
WEDNESDAY

"Now therefore, do not be afraid; I will provide for you and your little ones." And he comforted them and spoke kindly to them. —Genesis 50:21

MARCH
1
THURSDAY

Be of good comfort, be of one mind, live in peace; and the God of love and peace will be with you. —2 Corinthians 13:11

2
FRIDAY

Yea, though I walk through the valley of the shadow of death, I will fear no evil; for You are with me; Your rod and Your staff, they comfort me. —Psalm 23:4

3
SATURDAY

Blessed are those who mourn, for they shall be comforted. —Matthew 5:4

Dear Father,
For those who believe,
It is never late for love.
Indeed,
Love is not
A question of age,
It's a matter of readiness.
And the best way
To prepare ourselves
To receive
Is to give.
We know this, Lord,
For in loving You,
Our cup runneth over
With Your love.

KINDNESS

My daughter and I were putting final touches on posters when five-year-old Brett asked, "What's it say?"

"It says next week is Be Kind to Animals Week," his sister replied.

He was silent for a moment. "For one week? Then what happens the rest of the year? Is it Be Unkind to Animals time?"

Sometimes I find that my acts of kindness are mostly the planned or prompted kind: Our church pantry pleads for food; it's my turn to bake cookies for the nursing home. I sometimes forget that true kindness is more than isolated feats. Kindness is proof of God at work in us. Acts of kindness can be spontaneous and small: running an errand for a friend; scraping your neighbor's frosty windshield. Perhaps even leaving a little extra ham on that bone for your pooch.

So this month, I'm going to try harder to let my kindnesses be inspired by the Holy Spirit.

—Mary Lou Carney

❧ MARCH 2012 ❧

SUNDAY	MONDAY	TUESDAY	WEDNESDAY	THURSDAY	FRIDAY	SATURDAY
				1	2	3
4	5	6	7	8	9	10
11	12	13	14	15	16	17
18	19	20	21	22	23	24
25	26	27	28	29	30	31

Notes

FEBRUARY

S	M	T	W	T	F	S
			1	2	3	4
5	6	7	8	9	10	11
12	13	14	15	16	17	18
19	20	21	22	23	24	25
26	27	28	29			

APRIL

S	M	T	W	T	F	S
1	2	3	4	5	6	7
8	9	10	11	12	13	14
15	16	17	18	19	20	21
22	23	24	25	26	27	28
29	30					

Therefore, as the elect of God, holy and beloved, put on tender mercies, kindness, humility, meekness, longsuffering. —COLOSSIANS 3:12

Hey, Rug! Hey, Rug!" That's what Lil, an older homeless woman on my block calls my shaggy cocker spaniel Sally. Sally is usually willing to give Lil a friendly sniff as she goes about her morning business. For me, it's a little more complicated. Sometimes Lil asks for money. Since I know she will spend it on drink, I try not to give in.

Sometimes I'll buy her a muffin. Sometimes I give her the change in my pocket. But when it's raining and Sally's not cooperating, I simply walk on by, head down, not seeing the woman huddled under the dry cleaner's awning.

I never feel good about this. I tell myself I can't always help. And then I remember what my Aunt Marion used to say. "If you can be only one thing," she said, "be kind. God wants that most of all."

That's what unsettles me so much: I'm being unkind. Not by refusing to give Lil anything, but by ignoring her. There's always time for a "Good morning" or a wave. It's kind and it's what God wants me to do the next time I hear, "Hey, Rug! Hey, Rug!"

—Edward Grinnan

Prayer Requests _____

_____

_____

_____

Answered Prayers _____

_____

_____

_____

God's Touch _____

_____

_____

_____

4
SUNDAY

Blessed be the Lord, for He has shown me His marvelous kindness in a strong city! —Psalm 31:21

5
MONDAY

But You are God, ready to pardon, gracious and merciful, slow to anger, abundant in kindness, and did not forsake them. —Nehemiah 9:17

6
TUESDAY

For His merciful kindness is great toward us, and the truth of the Lord endures forever. —Psalm 117:2

7
WEDNESDAY

Add to your faith…brotherly kindness, and to brotherly kindness love. —2 Peter 1:5, 7

8
THURSDAY

"To him who is afflicted, kindness should be shown by his friend, even though he forsakes the fear of the Almighty." —Job 6:14

9
FRIDAY

But the fruit of the Spirit is love, joy, peace, longsuffering, kindness, goodness, faithfulness, gentleness, self-control. —Galatians 5:22, 23

10
SATURDAY

Return to the Lord your God, for He is gracious and merciful, slow to anger, and of great kindness. —Joel 2:13

I was in the middle of a particularly busy stretch at work—too many tasks, too few hours in the day. As the week dragged on and I got further and further behind, I grew increasingly short with my colleagues. "Nothing," I answered the first time someone asked what was wrong…and the second time and the third.

The fourth time I said something. "I think it's obvious I could use some help here, but I don't beg."

My colleague smiled. "Someone once told me that a Christian is a beggar telling another beggar where to find bread. We owe our lives to the generosity of someone else. Now how can I help you?"

There are certain things I know to be true about myself. I'm studious; I'm cautious; I'm conservative; I don't embrace change very easily. And I'm shy. I don't say a lot and certainly don't demand a lot from others.

I never thought that I would change—until that horribly busy week at work. That's when I learned I could be a little less self-reliant and a little more God-reliant, and even ask for help.

—Jeff Japinga

Prayer Requests _____
_____
_____
_____

Answered Prayers _____
_____
_____
_____

God's Touch _____
_____
_____
_____

11
SUNDAY

Give to everyone who asks of you. And from him who takes away your goods do not ask them back. —Luke 6:30

DAYLIGHT SAVING TIME BEGINS

12
MONDAY

Ask of Me, and I will give You the nations for Your inheritance, and the ends of the earth for Your possession. —Psalm 2:8

13
TUESDAY

If any of you lacks wisdom, let him ask of God, who gives to all liberally and without reproach, and it will be given to him. —James 1:5

14
WEDNESDAY

But let him ask in faith, with no doubting, for he who doubts is like a wave of the sea driven and tossed by the wind. —James 1:6

15
THURSDAY

"But now ask the beasts, and they will teach you; and the birds of the air, and they will tell you." —Job 12:7, 8

16
FRIDAY

If you abide in Me, and My words abide in you, you will ask what you desire, and it shall be done for you. —John 15:7

17
SATURDAY

If you then, being evil, know how to give good gifts to your children, how much more will your heavenly Father give the Holy Spirit to those who ask Him!" —Luke 11:13

ST. PATRICK'S DAY

Saturday was my parents' sixtieth wedding anniversary, so my four siblings and I planned a reception in their honor. Unfortunately, that Friday an ambulance ushered my father to a hospital fifteen miles away, and clouds threatened a rare Texas snowstorm. *How can we go on with it?* I thought. Yet how could we not? Family members were already en route from five hundred miles away.

So not only did I talk to God about the snowstorm, but I also talked to the storm itself. I took authority over it; I rebuked it; I spoke peace to it in the name of Jesus.

Still, it snowed four inches. Mixed with my discouragement was this one mental reminder from God: *Trust Me. I know how to bless my children.*

Amazingly, almost seventy people came! For three and a half hours friends and family ate, talked, laughed, hugged and wrote notes to Dad in the hospital.

God indeed knew how to bless His children. The glow of the evening stayed with Mother longer than the flowers they received. And the snow was a bonus that will bless her every time she remembers how people loved them enough to come in spite of it.

—Lucile Allen

Prayer Requests _____

_____

_____

_____

Answered Prayers _____

_____

_____

_____

God's Touch _____

_____

_____

_____

18
SUNDAY

For You, O Lord, will bless the righteous; with favor You will surround him as with a shield. —Psalm 5:12

19
MONDAY

For the Lord your God will bless you just as He promised you.... —Deuteronomy 15:6

20
TUESDAY

He who has a generous eye will be blessed, for he gives of his bread to the poor. —Proverbs 22:9
SPRING BEGINS

21
WEDNESDAY

My mouth shall speak the praise of the Lord, and all flesh shall bless His holy name forever and ever. —Psalm 145:21

22
THURSDAY

Blessed are the pure in heart, for they shall see God. —Matthew 5:8

23
FRIDAY

Bless those who curse you, and pray for those who spitefully use you. —Luke 6:28

24
SATURDAY

"The Lord bless you and keep you; the Lord make His face shine upon you, and be gracious to you...." —Numbers 6:24, 25

For whom the Lord loves He corrects,
just as a father the son in whom he delights. —PROVERBS 3:12

My son was searching the house for pencils to take a college entrance exam. "We must make a lot of mistakes," he said, laughing, "because all I can find are pencils with no erasers."

He had a point. I make my share of mistakes and not just when I'm writing. Last week, angry about a friend's criticism, I spoke too harshly to her. Now the friendship is in trouble. I regretted my words and wondered why I couldn't control my tongue. What does God do with mistake-makers? I asked myself.

Turning to the Bible, I was surprised to see that God puts His mistake-makers to work. The disciple Peter was devastated by his denying Jesus. But he went on to bring thousands to Christ. The Apostle Paul says he wants to do what is good but somehow can't seem to do it. Still, God used him to bring the Gospel to the entire Gentile world.

At least my house full of eraserless pencils show that we try to correct our mistakes. I needed to do that with my friend: apologize for being so quick-tempered. Maybe my mistake wouldn't mean the end of our friendship.

—Gina Bridgeman

Prayer Requests _____
_____
_____
_____

Answered Prayers _____
_____
_____
_____

God's Touch _____
_____
_____
_____

25
SUNDAY

Correct your son, and he will give you rest; yes, he will give delight to your soul.
—Proverbs 29:17

26
MONDAY

All Scripture is given by inspiration of God, and is profitable for doctrine, for reproof, for correction, for instruction in righteousness.... —2 Timothy 3:16

27
TUESDAY

"Shall the one who contends with the Almighty correct Him? He who rebukes God, let him answer it."
—Job 40:2

28
WEDNESDAY

We have all had human fathers who disciplined us and we respected them for it. How much more should we submit to the Father of spirits and live! —Hebrews 12:9 (NIV)

29
THURSDAY

Do not correct a scoffer, lest he hate you; rebuke a wise man, and he will love you. —Proverbs 9:8

30
FRIDAY

Preach the word; be prepared in season and out of season; correct, rebuke and encourage— with great patience and careful instruction. —2 Timothy 4:2 (NIV)

31
SATURDAY

He who keeps instruction is in the way of life, but he who refuses correction goes astray. —Proverbs 10:17

Dear Lord,
Walking on the beach
I can find an Easter message
Of hope
In a broken starfish.
Father,
Your sermons live in everything—
In deep, buried roots
Sending green shoots toward the sky;
In little ants bearing loads
Bigger than they are;
In the everyday marvels
Of bread dough rising,
And tadpoles changing into toads,
The warmth of the sun
Turning sour grapes sweet.
Open my eyes, Lord:
Your Word is not written
In books alone—
Help me see
That Your Sunday schoolroom
Is all around me
Every day.

ENTHUSIASM

*W*hy had I consented to chaperone this kindergarten field trip? Kids swarmed around me, jumping from seat to seat and bubbling with excitement.

Then we were on our way. Tiny faces pressed against the windows. "Look! A tractor!" Oohs and aahs drifted up from the seats. "A spider!" A daddy longlegs made his way down the aisle. How enthusiastic they were.

What about me? Was enthusiasm a quality I packed away? I went to my dictionary and discovered the word *enthusiasm* comes from two Greek words meaning "in God." The source of eagerness and excitement is no immaturity; it is the realization that God is at work in the world!

So this month I'll try to be more enthusiastic. I'll look forward to a few surprises: An early-spring picnic, a loving letter instead of a store-bought card. This month, I'm putting aside my indifference and stuffy maturity.

—Mary Lou Carney

❧ APRIL 2012 ❧

SUNDAY	MONDAY	TUESDAY	WEDNESDAY	THURSDAY	FRIDAY	SATURDAY
1	2	3	4	5	6	7
8	9	10	11	12	13	14
15	16	17	18	19	20	21
22	23	24	25	26	27	28
29	30					

Notes

MARCH

S	M	T	W	T	F	S
				1	2	3
4	5	6	7	8	9	10
11	12	13	14	15	16	17
18	19	20	21	22	23	24
25	26	27	28	29	30	31

MAY

S	M	T	W	T	F	S
		1	2	3	4	5
6	7	8	9	10	11	12
13	14	15	16	17	18	19
20	21	22	23	24	25	26
27	28	29	30	31		

After years of pain in a hip joint, I resigned myself to surgery.

Just six hours after the operation, the doctor had me sit up and then stand on the brand-new joint. There was pain from the eight-inch incision, but as I prepared for the deeper pain in my hip, there was nothing. "I can't believe it!" I said. "Why didn't I do this sooner?"

While I was recovering at home, some friends asked me to help with a problem they were having with a member of their work team. I spent hours on the phone and uncovered tremendous pain that had gone on for years.

On one of my laps around the couch, it hit me: *We need surgery here.* The old joint holding these people together needed to be cut out and something new put in its place.

Several people balked at the pain this "surgery" would cause, but weeks later, the team was well on its way to healing.

Do you have a pain where surgery will help? Why wait around while things only get worse? I promise you'll end up saying, "Why didn't I do this sooner?"

—Eric Fellman

Prayer Requests _____

_____

_____

_____

Answered Prayers _____

_____

_____

_____

_____

God's Touch _____

_____

_____

_____

1
SUNDAY

The blessing of the Lord brings wealth, without painful toil for it. —Proverbs 10:22 (NIV)
PALM SUNDAY

2
MONDAY

We know that the whole creation has been groaning as in the pains of childbirth right up to the present time. —Romans 8:22 (NIV)

3
TUESDAY

Now no chastening seems to be joyful for the present, but painful; nevertheless, afterward it yields the peaceable fruit of righteousness.... —Hebrews 12:11

4
WEDNESDAY

When I thought how to understand this, it was too painful for me—until I went into the sanctuary of God.... —Psalm 73:16, 17

5
THURSDAY

For it is commendable if someone bears up under the pain of unjust suffering because they are conscious of God. —1 Peter 2:19 (NIV)
MAUNDY THURSDAY

6
FRIDAY

He was despised and rejected by mankind, a man of suffering, and familiar with pain. —Isaiah 53:3 (NIV)
GOOD FRIDAY

7
SATURDAY

"There shall be no more pain, for the former things have passed away." —Revelation 21:4
HOLY SATURDAY / PASSOVER

According to John's Gospel, the women coming to anoint Jesus' body discovered the empty tomb. Peter and the beloved disciple ran to investigate. They found the grave clothes on the rock ledge of the tomb wall; only the face covering had been laid aside by itself. Perplexed, the disciples returned to their place of hiding.

When night came, the door to their secluded room was closed and bolted. Suddenly Jesus stood in their midst. The wounds of His Crucifixion could be clearly seen. He spoke to them and then disappeared.

The next day, He appeared to two of the disciples. Though they talked for hours as they hiked together, the disciples did not recognize Jesus. Only when they stopped at an inn for dinner did they identify Him by the unique way He blessed and broke the bread. Again, He disappeared.

Holy Week begins with the raising of Lazarus and ends with the Resurrection of Jesus, a mystery I can't possibly understand. But when I live in Easter faith, I learn that there are realities beyond my imagination, and that God is the Lord of life and death and all creation.

—Scott Walker

Prayer Requests _____

_____
_____
_____
_____

Answered Prayers _____

_____
_____
_____
_____

God's Touch _____

_____
_____
_____
_____

8
SUNDAY

So then, after the Lord had spoken to them, He was received up into heaven, and sat down at the right hand of God. —Mark 16:19

EASTER

9
MONDAY

For the Lord gives wisdom; from His mouth come knowledge and understanding. —Proverbs 2:6

10
TUESDAY

Then the cloud covered the tabernacle of meeting, and the glory of the Lord filled the tabernacle. —Exodus 40:34

11
WEDNESDAY

I will praise the Lord according to His righteousness, and will sing praise to the name of the Lord Most High. —Psalm 7:17

12
THURSDAY

Thomas answered and said to Him, "My Lord and my God!" —John 20:28

13
FRIDAY

But his delight is in the law of the Lord, and in His law he meditates day and night. —Psalm 1:2

14
SATURDAY

Watch therefore, for you do not know what hour your Lord is coming. —Matthew 24:42

Out of the ground the Lord God made every tree grow
that is pleasant to the sight and good for food. —GENESIS 2:9

*L*os Angeles is the largest city in the world built in a desert. So, when it rains several inches a day, and continues to do so on and off for a couple of weeks, the ground becomes saturated pretty fast. Runoff achieves mythic proportions as flash floods sweep down the control channels.

Yet, during all the drama of recent rainstorms, a small wonder in our front yard evoked more awe in my husband, Keith, and me than the forces of nature on a rampage: The dirt in which our roses grow became carpeted with moss. Looking at it, we felt a wonder born of nature's surprising lesson—that spores of the moss could hibernate in the desert ground for years without ever sprouting, and yet the potential to sprout was always there, under the surface.

God gives every growing thing the potential to sprout. We may lie dormant for a long time, but when conditions are right, we, like the humble, velvety green moss, can still appear, thrive and grow.

—Rhoda Blecker

Prayer Requests _____
_____
_____
_____
_____

Answered Prayers _____
_____
_____
_____
_____

God's Touch _____
_____
_____
_____
_____

15
SUNDAY

The righteous shall flourish like a palm tree, he shall grow like a cedar in Lebanon. —Psalm 92:12

16
MONDAY

The gospel is bearing fruit and growing throughout the whole world.... —Colossians 1:6 (NIV)

17
TUESDAY

"The seed will grow well, the vine will yield its fruit, the ground will produce its crops, and the heavens will drop their dew." —Zechariah 8:12 (NIV)

18
WEDNESDAY

"So why do you worry about clothing? Consider the lilies of the field, how they grow: they neither toil nor spin...." —Matthew 6:28

19
THURSDAY

Grow in the grace and knowledge of our Lord and Savior Jesus Christ. —2 Peter 3:18

20
FRIDAY

So neither the one who plants nor the one who waters is anything, but only God, who makes things grow. —1 Corinthians 3:7

21
SATURDAY

Let us not grow weary while doing good, for in due season we shall reap if we do not lose heart. —Galatians 6:9

During my seventy-three years I've experienced the deaths of many loved ones. Every time, I've noticed that, along with the grieving, I receive a precious gift—a renewed appreciation of life. I begin to notice things that I would normally take for granted.

Last week a friend and I had lunch at a nearby restaurant. During dessert, we noticed a tiny ladybug crawling across the table. Suddenly, we were immersed in a moment of great wonder as we watched her little body stop and carefully examine the crumb of chocolate cake I had placed in front of her. After opening and closing her little wings a couple of times as if preparing for takeoff, she tucked them back in again. She had decided to stay awhile.

I left the restaurant with a deep gladness and gratitude for this moment of great wonder and for life itself. And I wondered why I often tend to neglect the jewels of this very life, exactly as it is with all of its grief and ordinariness and enchantment.

—Marilyn Morgan King

Prayer Requests _____

_____

_____

_____

_____

Answered Prayers _____

_____

_____

_____

_____

God's Touch _____

_____

_____

_____

_____

22 SUNDAY

The Lord God formed man of the dust of the ground, and breathed into his nostrils the breath of life; and man became a living being. —Genesis 2:7

EARTH DAY

23 MONDAY

For the wages of sin is death, but the gift of God is eternal life in Christ Jesus our Lord. —Romans 6:23

24 TUESDAY

He who follows righteousness and mercy finds life, righteousness, and honor. —Proverbs 21:21

25 WEDNESDAY

You have granted me life and favor, and Your care has preserved my spirit. —Job 10:12

26 THURSDAY

I have come that they may have life, and that they may have it more abundantly. —John 10:10

27 FRIDAY

He who follows righteousness and mercy finds life, righteousness, and honor. —Proverbs 21:21

28 SATURDAY

"You have made known to me the ways of life; You will make me full of joy in Your presence." —Acts 2:28

Father God,
When tragedy
Strikes us down,
It is in fighting back
That You lift us up.
Lord, so often
We feel overwhelmed
By disappointments,
Mounting fears,
Physical pain.
Lord, grant us
The strength to endure,
The confidence to overcome,
The resolution to reach out,
The pluck to smile.
God, help us, too,
To choose life,
The life You give.
Lift us up!

It's mine! The red truck in mine!"

"I had it first! Let go!"

All morning I'd refereed squabbles in the playroom. I went down the hall, but when I pushed open the door, they were huddled over a puzzle.

I was touched by how quickly the children had forgiven each other. Was I that quick to forgive and forget? Didn't I sometimes hold onto my hurts?

Let's make this a month when we practice not holding grudges, when we refuse to be angry, when we distinctly forgive and forget. I will choose to be charitable instead of challenging.

—Mary Lou Carney

MAY 2012

SUNDAY	MONDAY	TUESDAY	WEDNESDAY	THURSDAY	FRIDAY	SATURDAY
		1	2	3	4	5
6	7	8	9	10	11	12
13	14	15	16	17	18	19
20	21	22	23	24	25	26
27	28	29	30	31		

Notes

APRIL

S	M	T	W	T	F	S
1	2	3	4	5	6	7
8	9	10	11	12	13	14
15	16	17	18	19	20	21
22	23	24	25	26	27	28
29	30					

JUNE

S	M	T	W	T	F	S
					1	2
3	4	5	6	7	8	9
10	11	12	13	14	15	16
17	18	19	20	21	22	23
24	25	26	27	28	29	30

Human life began in a garden; in the Song of Solomon, two people fall in love in a garden; Jesus was buried and rose again from a tomb in a garden.

Life, love, death and rebirth—all in a garden; to this my wife would say, "Of course." She'll soon retire from teaching and work in our garden all week. She'll harvest our garden next fall, until the first deep frost covers our crops and postpones paradise until the following spring. My wife doesn't need Bible references to know that a garden is good. The blessings of a well-tended one grow every day.

Last spring Rob and Paula, who own a ranch near us, gave us straw to use for garden mulch. In return I brought them some tomatoes in August. As a result of that visit, they and their youngest daughter came to church with us in September. The connection between their mulch and our tomatoes may not be direct, but it is very real. The connection between their generosity, our gratitude and worshipping God together may not be direct either, but it is just as real.

—Tim Williams

Prayer Requests _____

_____

_____

_____

_____

Answered Prayers _____

_____

_____

_____

_____

God's Touch _____

_____

_____

_____

_____

29 SUNDAY

And they heard the sound of the Lord God walking in the garden in the cool of the day.... —Genesis 3:8

30 MONDAY

My beloved has gone to his garden, to the beds of spices, to feed his flock in the gardens, and to gather lilies. —Song of Solomon 6:2

MAY

1 TUESDAY

They shall also make gardens and eat fruit from them. —Amos 9:14

2 WEDNESDAY

"It is like a mustard seed, which a man took and put in his garden; and it grew and became a large tree, and the birds of the air nested in its branches." —Luke 13:19

3 THURSDAY

I made myself gardens and orchards, and I planted all kinds of fruit trees in them. —Ecclesiastes 2:5

4 FRIDAY

Now in the place where He was crucified there was a garden, and in the garden a new tomb in which no one had yet been laid. —John 19:41

5 SATURDAY

You shall be like a watered garden, and like a spring of water, whose waters do not fail. —Isaiah 58:11

For hours I'd watched eight-year-old Alanzo wait patiently outside our makeshift clinic, an abandoned church with its interior divided by brightly colored sheets.

Every day that week, he had trekked two miles across the Belize countryside in hopes of finding relief from his headaches. Every day the eyeglasses they had ordered for him had been delayed.

On the final day of our two-week clinic the glasses arrived. Alanzo eagerly waited as I fished out his prescription and quickly fitted him with a pair of too-large frames that he would eventually grow into. He looked up at me through the lenses, his dark eyes magnified by the prescription. His face lit up and he began pointing. "I see you!" he shouted. Running around the churchyard, he exclaimed, "I see you, rock! I see you, tree!"

I held up a mirror so he could examine himself. He drew in a slow breath and whispered, "I see me."

I'm a long way from Belize now, but Alanzo's message has remained in my heart. There's a world of beauty all around me, if only I have eyes to see.

—Ashley Johnson

Prayer Requests _____

_____

_____

_____

Answered Prayers _____

_____

_____

_____

_____

God's Touch _____

_____

_____

_____

6
SUNDAY

Then He turned to His disciples and said privately, "Blessed are the eyes which see the things you see."
—Luke 10:23

7
MONDAY

In that day the deaf shall hear the words of the book, and the eyes of the blind shall see out of obscurity and out of darkness. —Isaiah 29:18

8
TUESDAY

"Now therefore, stand and see this great thing which the Lord will do before your eyes." —1 Samuel 12:16

9
WEDNESDAY

"But how he can see now, or who opened his eyes, we don't know. Ask him. He is of age; he will speak for himself." —John 9:21 (NIV)

10
THURSDAY

"His eyes are on the ways of man, and He sees all his steps." —Job 34:21

11
FRIDAY

Only take heed to yourself, and diligently keep yourself, lest you forget the things your eyes have seen.
—Deuteronomy 4:9

12
SATURDAY

Open my eyes, that I may see wondrous things from Your law. —Psalm 119:18

The lines have fallen to me in pleasant places; yes, I have a good inheritance. —PSALM 16:6

Following my mother's death, I found tucked in her Bible part of a handwritten note addressed to her. It was from a woman I didn't know, and it read in part:

"I love you for a number of reasons, the most important of which is what you did for my husband. When he was in the hospital, you visited him, though you'd never met him, and you encouraged several men in the church to visit him. As a result of those visits, my husband said, 'When I get better, I'm going to that church and find out what it has that makes those people so kind and lovable.' What he found, my dear friend, was Christ and Christian fellowship, neither of which he had known before."

It had been years since my mother was physically able to visit anyone, so I knew the letter was quite old. I folded it carefully and placed it back in her Bible.

How she must have treasured those words! What joy she must have experienced in the knowledge that she helped to introduce that man to Jesus! What a wonderful inheritance—and challenge—our Christian parents pass on to us.

—Drue Duke

Prayer Requests _____
_____
_____
_____

Answered Prayers _____
_____
_____
_____

God's Touch _____
_____
_____
_____

13
SUNDAY

Remember me, Lord...that I may share in the joy of your nation and join your inheritance in giving praise.
—Psalm 106:4, 5 (NIV)
MOTHER'S DAY

14
MONDAY

By faith Abraham, when called to go to a place he would later receive as his inheritance, obeyed and went....
—Hebrews 11:8

15
TUESDAY

A good man leaves an inheritance to his children's children, but the wealth of the sinner is stored up for the righteous. —Proverbs 13:22

16
WEDNESDAY

"Then the King will say to those on his right, 'Come, you who are blessed by my Father; take your inheritance.'"
—Matthew 25:34

17
THURSDAY

Whatever you do, do it heartily, as to the Lord and not to men, knowing that from the Lord you will receive the reward of the inheritance. —Colossians 3:23, 24

18
FRIDAY

For the Lord will not reject his people; he will never forsake his inheritance. —Psalm 94:14

19
SATURDAY

An inheritance claimed too soon will not be blessed at the end. —Proverbs 20:21 (NIV)

When Keith and I first discussed moving out of Los Angeles after he retired, I had mixed feelings. I was not so wedded to the city, but I loved our home. We'd remodeled it so that it was exactly what we wanted, and it was really the only house I'd ever lived in where I was altogether happy. The idea of selling it made me uneasy. "I think of our home as a place of safety, a place that surrounds me with its walls and holds me gently," I said. "I'm afraid to go away from it."

Keith smiled, the way he does when I get frantic over something and he has to point to the terra-cotta plaque on our wall that reads: "Be still, and know that I am God." Keith said, "It's not the house that shelters you."

And I knew that he was right. It was God Who held me safely when I was at home—and also when I went away from it. And God would continue to shelter me, whether I lived in Los Angeles or anywhere else.

—Rhoda Blecker

Prayer Requests

Answered Prayers

God's Touch

20
SUNDAY

[The cloud] will be a shelter and shade from the heat of the day, and a refuge and hiding place from the storm and rain. —Isaiah 4:6 (NIV)

21
MONDAY

The Lord is a shelter for the oppressed, a refuge in times of trouble. —Psalm 9:9 (NLT)

22
TUESDAY

For in the day of trouble he will keep me safe in his dwelling; he will hide me in the shelter of his sacred tent and set me high upon a rock. —Psalm 27:5 (NIV)

23
WEDNESDAY

He who sits on the throne will give them shelter. —Revelation 7:15 (NLT)

24
THURSDAY

I would hurry to my place of shelter, far from the tempest and storm. —Psalm 55:8 (NIV)

25
FRIDAY

The heavens and earth will shake; but the Lord will be a shelter for His people. —Joel 3:16

26
SATURDAY

Deliver me, O Lord, from my enemies; in You I take shelter. —Psalm 143:9

At the restaurant where I like to eat breakfast, the waitresses have stars on their aprons to tell you how many years they've been dishing up oatmeal and toting plates of bacon and eggs for their clientele. Some wear three or four stars; this morning my waitress Trina boasted six stars.

As I left, filled with biscuits and gravy just like my mother used to make, I saw a young woman coming out of the kitchen. She couldn't have been much out of her teens. She was wearing the brown apron of a waitress, and I checked for the brightly embroidered stars. Where they would have been were two words in bold script: **Rising Star**. Not *Beginner* or *Trainee*. Not *New* or *Inexperienced*. Not *Good-Luck-with-Getting-Your Order-Right*. *Rising Star*, an affirmation of what they were expecting her to become: competent, efficient, outstanding.

I left the restaurant determined to give everyone the benefit of believing they can accomplish great things. Everyone—even me!

—Mary Lou Carney

Prayer Requests

Answered Prayers

God's Touch

27
SUNDAY

He does great things past finding out, yes, wonders without number. —Job 9:10

28
MONDAY

"Go home to your friends, and tell them what great things the Lord has done for you, and how He has had compassion on you." —Mark 5:19
MEMORIAL DAY

29
TUESDAY

Then Saul said to David, "May you be blessed, David my son; you will do great things and surely triumph." —1 Samuel 26:25 (NIV)

30
WEDNESDAY

"Call to Me, and I will answer you, and show you great and mighty things, which you do not know." —Jeremiah 33:3

31
THURSDAY

Don't be afraid, my people. Be glad now and rejoice, for the Lord has done great things. —Joel 2:21 (NLT)

JUNE
1
FRIDAY

And Stephen, full of faith and power, did great wonders and signs among the people. —Acts 6:8

2
SATURDAY

Only fear the Lord, and serve Him in truth with all your heart; for consider what great things He has done for you. —1 Samuel 12:24

Heavenly Father,
We're so proud
Of young people today!
They're scrappy,
Sensitive,
Trying hard
To work out what's right.
To live the way You taught us.
For many of them
It's commencement time.
But though classes may be over,
This is no ending:
The confusing times,
The questioning, uncertain times
Are now commencing.
Lord, help us to help them
As they get their béarings,
Set their goals,
Work steadfastly
Toward the only prizes that really matter:
Yours.

CREATIVITY

You can make anything you want," the teacher said, placing jars of paint on each table. The preschoolers dipped their fingers into pots of blue, red, green and yellow. They began swiping and swirling the colors across their papers.

When the pictures were finally done, we arranged them: a strawberry tree, purple grass, a blue dog and a lady with six hands, "because my mommy's always saying she needs more hands!"

How routine my own life had become! I made the same meat loaf. I drove the same routes. I prayed the same phrases. I even made the same mistakes.

God is the great Creator—creativity is our heritage. This month, I'll practice creativity. Skip instead of plod. Draw a few strawberry trees.

—Mary Lou Carney

JUNE 2012

SUNDAY	MONDAY	TUESDAY	WEDNESDAY	THURSDAY	FRIDAY	SATURDAY
					1	2
3	4	5	6	7	8	9
10	11	12	13	14	15	16
17	18	19	20	21	22	23
24	25	26	27	28	29	30

Notes

MAY

S	M	T	W	T	F	S
		1	2	3	4	5
6	7	8	9	10	11	12
13	14	15	16	17	18	19
20	21	22	23	24	25	26
27	28	29	30	31		

JULY

S	M	T	W	T	F	S
1	2	3	4	5	6	7
8	9	10	11	12	13	14
15	16	17	18	19	20	21
22	23	24	25	26	27	28
29	30	31				

I love the first few mentally uncluttered moments of morning when my thoughts, often reruns from the day before, come one at a time and stay for a little visit.

You could have corrected her a little more kindly, one thought says about my eleven-year-old daughter. I ask God to forgive me, to help me be gentler, and then promise myself I'll ask her forgiveness, too.

Why couldn't you have hugged Mrs. Doyle before leaving the nursing home yesterday? So what if it is a little out of your comfort zone? says another thought as I picture this dear lady sitting by the bed of the love of her life and husband of sixty-two years. She's waiting to see if he will pull through this latest setback after a stroke and probably wondering how she'll go on without him if he doesn't. Surely a hug would have comforted Mrs. Doyle.

There was a time when these early morning memories would have settled on my mind like condemning black clouds and darkened my mood for days. Today I embrace them as gentle reminders from Jesus on how to live—and love—a little better.

—Lucile Allen

Prayer Requests _____

_____
_____
_____
_____

Answered Prayers _____

_____
_____
_____
_____
_____

God's Touch _____

_____
_____
_____
_____

3
SUNDAY

Now in the morning, having risen a long while before daylight, He went out and departed to a solitary place; and there He prayed. —Mark 1:35

4
MONDAY

He awakens me morning by morning, He awakens my ear to hear as the learned. —Isaiah 50:4

5
TUESDAY

I rise before the dawning of the morning, and cry for help; I hope in Your word. —Psalm 119:147

6
WEDNESDAY

Then early in the morning all the people came to Him in the temple to hear Him. —Luke 21:38

7
THURSDAY

Through the Lord's mercies we are not consumed, because His compassions fail not. They are new every morning; great is Your faithfulness. —Lamentations 3:22, 23

8
FRIDAY

O Lord, be gracious to us; we have waited for You. Be their arm every morning, our salvation also in the time of trouble. —Isaiah 33:2

9
SATURDAY

My voice You shall hear in the morning, O Lord; in the morning I will direct it to You, and I will look up. —Psalm 5:3

For to this you were called, because Christ also suffered for us,
leaving us an example, that you should follow His steps. —1 PETER 2:21

I can't think about the Bible for very long without remembering Grandma Fellman. She lived to be ninety-eight and kept her Bible beside her always.

Years ago her elderly daughter, my aunt, sent me that Bible. Its leather cover is worn and tattered, and some of the pages have come loose from the binding. People have suggested that I have it restored, but I like it the way it is. Holding it with the spine in my palm, I can feel the impression of Grandma's hand. She held it that way with me on her lap and her arms around me.

She often told me, "Honey, this book is about one thing: the Savior Jesus. The old part is about how we lost touch with God and He made a plan to send Jesus to bring us back. The new part tells Jesus' life story and how He wants us to live. Follow His way and you will never go wrong."

I hope Grandma tells Jesus that lots of us down here are trying to follow His way and she'll ask Him to keep being patient with us.

—Eric Fellman

Prayer Requests _____

_____

_____

_____

Answered Prayers _____

_____

_____

_____

God's Touch _____

_____

_____

_____

10
SUNDAY

Now it happened as they journeyed on the road, that someone said to Him, "Lord, I will follow You wherever You go." —Luke 9:57

11
MONDAY

"My sheep hear My voice, and I know them, and they follow Me." —John 10:27

12
TUESDAY

It is the Lord your God you must follow, and him you must revere. Keep his commands and obey him; serve him and hold fast to him. —Deuteronomy 13:4 (NIV)

13
WEDNESDAY

Then Jesus said to His disciples, "If anyone desires to come after Me, let him deny himself, and take up his cross, and follow Me." —Matthew 16:24

14
THURSDAY

Surely goodness and mercy shall follow me all the days of my life; and I will dwell in the house of the Lord forever. —Psalm 23:6
FLAG DAY

15
FRIDAY

"You shall follow what is altogether just, that you may live and inherit the land which the Lord your God is giving you." —Deuteronomy 16:20

16
SATURDAY

Teach me, Lord, the way of your decrees, that I may follow it to the end. —Psalm 119:33 (NIV)

I will both lie down in peace, and sleep; for You alone,
O Lord, make me dwell in safety. —PSALM 4:8

 I'd noticed that problems that didn't bother me during daylight suddenly loomed larger between midnight and 5:00 AM, things like *Who'll I find to teach my Sunday school class when we go on vacation? What if Social Security benefits run out? Where is that "safe place" I hid the key so I'd be sure not to lose it?*

Finally, I confided these concerns to Sarah, one of my friends. "All these who-what-when-where-whys keep me awake. I don't recall losing sleep over such matters when I was a child."

Sarah chuckled. "When we were children, we simply expected our parents to take care of everything. That's why we didn't worry back then."

"But you seem so calm, so serene. And you don't have parents anymore, either."

"Oh, but I do," she answered. "I have a heavenly Father Who's promised to watch over me. He says He doesn't slumber or sleep. So at bedtime I simply turn my troubles over to Him. You see, He's going to stay up all night anyway, so why should I?"

—Isabel Wolseley

Prayer Requests _____

_____

_____

_____

Answered Prayers _____

_____

_____

_____

God's Touch _____

_____

_____

_____

17
SUNDAY

"Look at the birds of the air, for they neither sow nor reap nor gather into barns; yet your heavenly Father feeds them. Are you not of more value than they?" —Matthew 6:26
FATHER'S DAY

18
MONDAY

After this I awoke and looked around, and my sleep was sweet to me. —Jeremiah 31:26

19
TUESDAY

Blessed be the God and Father of our Lord Jesus Christ, who has blessed us with every spiritual blessing in the heavenly places in Christ. —Ephesians 1:3

20
WEDNESDAY

The righteous cry out, and the Lord hears, and delivers them out of all their troubles. —Psalm 34:17
SUMMER BEGINS

21
THURSDAY

When you lie down, you will not be afraid; yes, you will lie down and your sleep will be sweet. —Proverbs 3:24

22
FRIDAY

It is vain for you to rise up early, to sit up late, to eat the bread of sorrows; for so He gives His beloved sleep. —Psalm 127:2

23
SATURDAY

Then Jesus said to them, "Most assuredly, I say to you, Moses did not give you the bread from heaven, but My Father gives you the true bread from heaven." —John 6:32

Ruby is my Eskimo granddaughter, welcomed to our daughter Tamara's family when she was two days old. Now she is a grinning, bright-eyed four-year-old who says she is "Eksimo."

One day, while working with Ruby and her siblings on the subject of patience, I grouped the letters in the word *patient* and converted it to a singsong chant. "*PA-TI-ENT*," I called. "What does that spell?"

Ruby enthusiastically shouted, "Patient!"

"What does *patient* mean?" I asked.

In her best four-year-old pronunciation she explained, "It means waiting without *cwying*."

Ruby wasn't satisfied just to know the definition; she wanted to learn to spell the word. She practiced over and over. Her tongue continually stumbled and tripped, but she stayed with it. "PI."

"No, it's PATI," I corrected.

"PATAENT."

"Oh, you're close. Remember, PATI."

Ruby tried once more, heard herself make a mistake, good-naturedly proclaimed, "I messed up again," and started over.

The day came when she got it right and we whooped it up. She may not remember her achievement down the line, but I'll never forget the day I watched my Eskimo granddaughter patiently work to spell *patient*.

—Carol Knapp

Prayer Requests _____

_____

_____

Answered Prayers _____

_____

_____

God's Touch _____

_____

_____

24
SUNDAY

Now we exhort you, brethren, warn those who are unruly, comfort the fainthearted, uphold the weak, be patient with all. —1 Thessalonians 5:14

25
MONDAY

See how the farmer waits for the precious fruit of the earth, waiting patiently for it until it receives the early and latter rain. —James 5:7

26
TUESDAY

Rest in the Lord, and wait patiently for Him. —Psalm 37:7

27
WEDNESDAY

But when you do good and suffer, if you take it patiently, this is commendable before God. —1 Peter 2:20

28
THURSDAY

And so, after he had patiently endured, he obtained the promise. —Hebrews 6:15

29
FRIDAY

A hot-tempered person stirs up conflict, but the one who is patient calms a quarrel. —Proverbs 15:18

30
SATURDAY

I waited patiently for the Lord; and He inclined to me, and heard my cry. —Psalm 40:1

Dear Heavenly Father,
We've seen Your closeness
To those in need;
We've felt Your Presence
In a country kitchen;
You were there in a boat adrift,
Holding a young, frightened sailor;
You marched beside
An embarrassed little boy
Limping through an Independence parade.
Now be with us, too, we pray,
In our summer celebrations.
Sail with us across Your bays,
Climb with us Your towering mountains;
And watch with us the spangled sprays
Of fireworks,
Commemorating the freedom
You helped us win.

AFFECTION

Dawn and Brandy worship with me every Sunday. They are "bus children" who come to church without their parents. We sit close, share a hymnal. We hold hands during the sermon. They smile whenever I glance their ways and after service come the hugs.

Dawn and Brandy teach me the importance of affection. True affection. The reaching out that makes tangible the fact that they care for me. How often I stifle that in my other relationships! But it doesn't have to be that way. Affection is God's gift to us and to each other. We can show it in concerned phone calls, in impromptu postcards. We can learn to touch the lives of those most dear to us, and be touched and renewed ourselves.

I'm going to throw off dry decorum. I'm going to find ways to show affection to those I care about and to make myself available to receive it as well.

—Mary Lou Carney

JULY 2012

SUNDAY	MONDAY	TUESDAY	WEDNESDAY	THURSDAY	FRIDAY	SATURDAY
1	2	3	4	5	6	7
8	9	10	11	12	13	14
15	16	17	18	19	20	21
22	23	24	25	26	27	28
29	30	31				

Notes

JUNE

S	M	T	W	T	F	S
					1	2
3	4	5	6	7	8	9
10	11	12	13	14	15	16
17	18	19	20	21	22	23
24	25	26	27	28	29	30

AUGUST

S	M	T	W	T	F	S
			1	2	3	4
5	6	7	8	9	10	11
12	13	14	15	16	17	18
19	20	21	22	23	24	25
26	27	28	29	30	31	

Let's just say my house was untidy the morning I turned the radio dial to a station celebrating "Christmas in July." By late afternoon they'd played one carol four times: "Joy to the world, the Lord is come." Each time I heard one line as if it were a command: "Let every heart prepare Him room." I was puzzled. Lord, how do I "prepare You room"?

That evening I invited friends over for dinner the following night. Next day I emptied wastebaskets and discarded clutter. I vacuumed, wiped and washed. I even rubbed a shine onto silver iced-tea spoons I had neglected. Finally I brought in fresh groceries, which I served on a table set with extra plates, surrounded by extra chairs.

When my guests knocked on the door, I was ready with a hearty welcome and some new practices in my spiritual life: Discard the unsightly. Value the good. Clean the dirty. Tend the true. Bring in the fresh. Make room for a guest.

—Evelyn Bence

Prayer Requests _____

_____

_____

_____

_____

Answered Prayers _____

_____

_____

_____

_____

God's Touch _____

_____

_____

_____

_____

1
SUNDAY

Lord, You have heard the desire of the humble; You will prepare their heart; You will cause Your ear to hear. —Psalm 10:17

2
MONDAY

If anyone cleanses himself…he will be a vessel for honor, sanctified and useful for the Master, prepared for every good work. —2 Timothy 2:21

3
TUESDAY

"This is he of whom it is written: 'Behold, I send My messenger before Your face, who will prepare Your way before You.'" —Luke 7:27

4
WEDNESDAY

How can a young man cleanse his way? By taking heed according to Your word. —Psalm 119:9
INDEPENDENCE DAY

5
THURSDAY

Draw near to God and He will draw near to you. Cleanse your hands, you sinners; and purify your hearts, you double-minded. —James 4:8

6
FRIDAY

Now Hezekiah commanded them to prepare rooms in the house of the Lord, and they prepared them. —2 Chronicles 31:11

7
SATURDAY

Create in me a clean heart, O God, and renew a steadfast spirit within me. —Psalm 51:10

He stilled the storm to a whisper; the waves of the sea were hushed. —PSALM 107:29 (NIV)

Beau is my ninety-pound golden retriever. Every day we greet the new morning together and each night we take long walks. I guess you could say we're best friends.

Tonight, Beau is sprawled on the study floor next to my desk. Outside, a thunderstorm rages, and Beau is nervous. Twice in the last five minutes he has stood up and placed his wide muzzle on my leg, demanding that I ruffle his ears and pat him on the head. And when I stop, he lifts his paw for me to hold. He can't be touched enough.

I guess I'm a lot like Beau. When I walk through my own storms, God just can't be near enough to me. I need reassurance that He is bigger than the storm.

Tonight as I help Beau through his troubled moments, I'm reassured that God's love and care for me dwarfs my own compassion. Though sometimes I don't feel God's hand on my shoulder, He's always there. And He has promised me that there's no storm He and I can't live through together.

—Scott Walker

Prayer Requests _____

_____

_____

Answered Prayers _____

_____

_____

_____

God's Touch _____

_____

_____

8
SUNDAY

He stirs up the sea with His power, and by His understanding He breaks up the storm. —Job 26:12

9
MONDAY

The Lord has His way in the whirlwind and in the storm, and the clouds are the dust of His feet. —Nahum 1:3

10
TUESDAY

For You have been a strength to the poor, a strength to the needy in his distress, a refuge from the storm, a shade from the heat. —Isaiah 25:4

11
WEDNESDAY

When the storm has swept by, the wicked are gone, but the righteous stand firm forever. —Proverbs 10:25 (NIV)

12
THURSDAY

Suddenly a furious storm came up on the lake, so that the waves swept over the boat. But Jesus was sleeping. —Matthew 8:24 (NIV)

13
FRIDAY

You rule the oceans. You subdue their storm-tossed waves. —Psalm 89:9 (NLT)

14
SATURDAY

Then the Lord spoke to Job out of the storm. —Job 40:6

It was the highlight of my trip to Rome: St. Peter's Basilica. "And that is the Pietà," said our guide, gesturing toward the far wall, where Michelangelo's famous sculpture stood. I stared at Mary holding the body of her son, newly taken down from the Cross. The piece seemed to glow with a light that came from inside the marble. I was drawn to it with a force I could barely contain.

Leaving the tour group, I headed for the small altar in front of the work. Before I got there, I began to cry. Such passion! Such sadness! And yet the look on Mary's face…what was it? Sorrow, certainly, but something else too.

I became aware of a shoulder touching mine. I looked into the face of an Italian woman about my age. Our eyes met. She was crying too. She reached for my hand, and together we prayed. I looked full into the face of Mary, and suddenly I recognized what the look on her face was. *Hope.* She knew that evil would not have the final say. She knew it as surely as she knew her own Son.

—Mary Lou Carney

Prayer Requests _____

_____

_____

_____

_____

Answered Prayers _____

_____

_____

_____

_____

God's Touch _____

_____

_____

_____

_____

15
SUNDAY

It is good that one should hope and wait quietly for the salvation of the Lord. —Lamentations 3:26

16
MONDAY

And everyone who has this hope in Him purifies himself, just as He is pure. —1 John 3:3

17
TUESDAY

"Blessed is the man who trusts in the Lord, and whose hope is the Lord." —Jeremiah 17:7

18
WEDNESDAY

Hope deferred makes the heart sick, but when the desire comes, it is a tree of life. —Proverbs 13:12

19
THURSDAY

Let us hold fast the confession of our hope without wavering, for He who promised is faithful. —Hebrews 10:23

20
FRIDAY

Why are you cast down, O my soul? And why are you disquieted within me? Hope in God, for I shall yet praise Him for the help of His countenance. —Psalm 42:5

21
SATURDAY

Let us who are of the day be sober, putting on the breastplate of faith and love, and as a helmet the hope of salvation. —1 Thessalonians 5:8

During my junior year of college, my parents called to tell me that they'd found a new house for us and during summer break we'd be moving. At first I was excited, but as we continued to discuss the move I started to worry. *Will I have enough space in my new bedroom? What is the new neighborhood like?*

After hanging up, I sat down and stared at the walls of my small apartment. My worries began to snowball. *Where will I live next year at college? Can I get an apartment near friends? And what about after graduation? What kind of job will I get and where will I live? I could end up halfway across the country!*

This absurdity went on for days until one morning when I read the story of Joseph in the book of Genesis. When he's sold into slavery, a certain phrase is used: "The Lord was with him."

Those words reminded me that no matter where I ended up geographically, I could rest assured that God would be there too. The only thing I'd have to worry about was meeting the new neighbors.

—Joshua Sundquist

Prayer Requests _____

_____

_____

_____

Answered Prayers _____

_____

_____

_____

_____

God's Touch _____

_____

_____

_____

_____

22
SUNDAY

All those who heard them kept them in their hearts, saying, "What kind of child will this be?" And the hand of the Lord was with him. —Luke 1:66

23
MONDAY

The hand of the Lord was with them, and a great number believed and turned to the Lord. —Acts 11:21

24
TUESDAY

And David behaved wisely in all his ways, and the Lord was with him. —1 Samuel 18:14

25
WEDNESDAY

So the Lord was with Joshua, and his fame spread throughout all the country. —Joshua 6:27

26
THURSDAY

Grace, mercy, and peace will be with you from God the Father and from the Lord Jesus Christ, the Son of the Father, in truth and love. —2 John 1:3

27
FRIDAY

As Samuel grew up, the Lord was with him, and everything Samuel said proved to be reliable. —1 Samuel 3:19 (NLT)

28
SATURDAY

The Lord appeared to him the same night and said, "I am the God of your father Abraham; do not fear, for I am with you." —Genesis 26:24

We spend these long summer days,
With family, with loved ones,
But remembering too,
Those who are gone.
In the lingering twilight, we recall with love
And are assured that they rest
With You.
And we enjoy the warmth, the light
The love of family and of You.

LAUGHTER

Knock-knock."
   "Who's there?"
"Wanda."
"Wanda who?"
"Wanda who thinks up these jokes?"

The girls broke into giggles, doubling up on the bunks and kicking their bare feet in glee. It was "laugh night" in my cabin, and the campers were making the most of it.

Long after the girls were asleep, I lay awake, remembering the laughter-lit eyes of the children. Such silly humor! But what catharsis it had been for all of us. Homesickness vanished, hurt feelings healed, tired spirits rallied. I realized how seldom I applied this "medicine" to my own life. This month I'm going to laugh more—at silly movies, with old friends. I'll even laugh at myself, and thank God for the gift of laughter.

—Mary Lou Carney

AUGUST 2012

SUNDAY	MONDAY	TUESDAY	WEDNESDAY	THURSDAY	FRIDAY	SATURDAY
			1	2	3	4
5	6	7	8	9	10	11
12	13	14	15	16	17	18
19	20	21	22	23	24	25
26	27	28	29	30	31	

Notes

JULY

S	M	T	W	T	F	S
1	2	3	4	5	6	7
8	9	10	11	12	13	14
15	16	17	18	19	20	21
22	23	24	25	26	27	28
29	30	31				

SEPTEMBER

S	M	T	W	T	F	S
						1
2	3	4	5	6	7	8
9	10	11	12	13	14	15
16	17	18	19	20	21	22
23/30	24	25	26	27	28	29

And the earth was without form and void;
and darkness was upon the face of the deep…. —GENESIS 1:2

I first came across the phrase *tohu va-vohu* in Professor Everett Fox's translation of the Book of Genesis. Better known to most Bible readers as "without form and void," the words are the original Hebrew description of the condition of the earth at the time of creation.

There's something thrilling to me about the way the sound of these alien words conjures up the state of things before God set to building and ordering the universe. Fox translates the words as "wild and waste," emphasizing that in the Hebrew, there is a suggestion that in the course of creation God brings order out of a condition of chaos.

Tohu va-vohu. When I'm confronted with chaos in my own life—whether in the form of a messy apartment or a scene of violence and devastation on the evening news—I often find these Hebrew syllables coming to mind. To me, they serve as a reminder that all the beauty and order in the world began from an absence of those qualities, and that, where chaos seems to reign, a seed of order and goodness is waiting, with God's help, to be brought forth.

—Ptolemy Tompkins

Prayer Requests _____

_____

_____

_____

Answered Prayers _____

_____

_____

_____

God's Touch _____

_____

_____

_____

He has made everything beautiful in its time. —Ecclesiastes 3:11

29
SUNDAY

The creation itself also will be delivered from the bondage of corruption into the glorious liberty of the children of God. —Romans 8:21

30
MONDAY

Let the beauty of the Lord our God be upon us, and establish the work of our hands for us; yes, establish the work of our hands. —Psalm 90:17

31
TUESDAY

"Dominion and awe belong to God; he establishes order in the heights of heaven." —Job 25:2 (NIV)

AUGUST
1
WEDNESDAY

By faith we understand that the universe was formed at God's command, so that what is seen was not made out of what was visible. —Hebrews 11:3 (NIV)

2
THURSDAY

Therefore, if anyone is in Christ, he is a new creation; old things have passed away; behold, all things have become new. —2 Corinthians 5:17

3
FRIDAY

My lips shall greatly rejoice when I sing to You, and my soul, which You have redeemed. —Psalm 71:23

4
SATURDAY

It's Sunday morning and I'd love to be in church. But my aunt is recovering from an upper respiratory infection. As a child she survived a notorious influenza epidemic. Now, at one hundred years old, she seems to have won another round. She is weak and tired; I don't dare leave her, even for an hour. So feeling shut in, I sit and stare out my bedroom window. A song sparrow bursts into melody in the branches of a Chinese elm.

Quietly, a new awareness comes to me. Hadn't I stepped outside this morning in the predawn to gaze at the stars? Do the candles in church glow more brightly than these? Hadn't I gone out again when the rising sun tinted the clouds pink? Are stained-glass windows more vibrant with color? And this songbird in the tree—will the choir's anthem sing more gloriously to God?

As for missing the Sunday message, didn't Jesus say, "Be ye therefore merciful, as your Father also is merciful" (Luke 6:36)? My aunt needs mercy today. By being here with her, I'm not hearing a sermon—I'm living one.

—Carol Knapp

Prayer Requests _____

_____

_____

_____

Answered Prayers _____

_____

_____

_____

God's Touch _____

_____

_____

_____

5
SUNDAY

"Thus says the Lord of hosts: 'Execute true justice, show mercy and compassion everyone to his brother.'"
—Zechariah 7:9

6
MONDAY

Let not mercy and truth forsake you; bind them around your neck, write them on the tablet of your heart.
—Proverbs 3:3

7
TUESDAY

Your mercy, O Lord, is in the heavens; Your faithfulness reaches to the clouds. —Psalm 36:5

8
WEDNESDAY

Therefore, since we have this ministry, as we have received mercy, we do not lose heart. —2 Corinthians 4:1

9
THURSDAY

Oh, satisfy us early with Your mercy, that we may rejoice and be glad all our days! —Psalm 90:14

10
FRIDAY

Let us therefore come boldly to the throne of grace, that we may obtain mercy and find grace to help in time of need. —Hebrews 4:16

11
SATURDAY

Oh, give thanks to the Lord, for He is good! For His mercy endures forever. —1 Chronicles 16:34

I was having lunch in a local steakhouse when a teenage girl came stomping in behind a man who appeared to be her father. I read the neon green lettering on her black shirt: PRETEND I'M NOT HERE. THAT'S WHAT I'M DOING.

But as my eyes traveled upward to braces and a sprinkle of acne, I noticed the most gorgeous auburn hair pulled back into a ponytail. *If she didn't have such an attitude, I'd compliment her.*

Just then, I sensed a prompting: Do it anyway. *You'll pass her on your way to the salad bar. Her T-shirt is a cry for help.* I tapped the girl on the shoulder and heard myself stammer, "You have the most beautiful hair." She glared back at me, and words I never planned rolled off my tongue. "You must hear that a lot."

"No, never," she answered, a startled look on her face. And then she smiled—a sweet "I forgot I'm wearing braces" smile. When I returned with my salad, words between the girl and the man were tumbling out in a flurry of conversation. From the table behind them, I prayed, "Lord, help me never to be fooled by a message on a T-shirt."

—Roberta Messner

Prayer Requests _____

_____

_____

_____

Answered Prayers _____

_____

_____

_____

God's Touch _____

_____

_____

_____

12
SUNDAY

Do you judge uprightly, you sons of men? —Psalm 58:1

13
MONDAY

Therefore give to Your servant an understanding heart to judge Your people, that I may discern between good and evil. —1 Kings 3:9

14
TUESDAY

Let us not judge one another anymore, but rather resolve this, not to put a stumbling block or a cause to fall in our brother's way. —Romans 14:13

15
WEDNESDAY

"Do not judge according to appearance, but judge with righteous judgment." —John 7:24

16
THURSDAY

But be doers of the word, and not hearers only, deceiving yourselves. —James 1:22

17
FRIDAY

My little children, let us not love in word or in tongue, but in deed and in truth. —1 John 3:18

18
SATURDAY

Pleasant words are like a honeycomb, sweetness to the soul and health to the bones. —Proverbs 16:24

They shall still bear fruit in old age; they shall be fresh and flourishing. —PSALM 92:14

I feel a little foolish, planting trees at my age. I won't live long enough to see them mature. I planted forty trees on our new property, and it's the hardest work I've ever done, digging out rock-hard clay and then filling the hole with black dirt, using only a shovel and a wheelbarrow. Only then could I plant the tree and expect it to survive.

White oaks grow very slowly, but they can live four hundred years. The ginkgos may be the slowest growing tree in the world. It is called the "Tree of Hope" because some of them survived the blast at Hiroshima. Its beauty is worth the wait.

Why am I planting trees whose shade I might never enjoy? For one thing, I have learned late in life that things can happen if I just get started. Furthermore, even if I don't live to see the trees full-grown, my children and grandchildren will enjoy the fruit of my labors.

I don't think there's any law that says people have to finish everything they begin. Old age is a good time to start things that will outlive me.

—Daniel Schantz

Prayer Requests _____

_____

_____

_____

Answered Prayers _____

_____

_____

_____

God's Touch _____

_____

_____

_____

19
SUNDAY

Wisdom is with aged men, and with length of days, understanding. —Job 12:12

20
MONDAY

A good tree cannot bear bad fruit, nor can a bad tree bear good fruit. —Matthew 7:18

21
TUESDAY

You did not choose Me, but I chose you and appointed you that you should go and bear fruit, and that your fruit should remain. —John 15:16

22
WEDNESDAY

I have been young, and now am old; yet I have not seen the righteous forsaken, nor his descendants begging bread. —Psalm 37:25

23
THURSDAY

Even to your old age, I am He, and even to gray hairs I will carry you! —Isaiah 46:4

24
FRIDAY

Every branch in Me that does not bear fruit He takes away; and every branch that bears fruit He prunes, that it may bear more fruit. —John 15:2

25
SATURDAY

Do not cast me off in the time of old age; do not forsake me when my strength fails. —Psalm 71:9

Do you not know that a little leaven leavens the whole lump? —1 CORINTHIANS 5:6

A sentence typed like this is useless: *Mpe od yjr yo,r gpt s;; hppf ,rm yp vp,r yp yjr sof pg yjrot vpimytu/.*

But if I move my hands just one letter to the left on my keyboard, this familiar phrase is easily read: *Now is the time for all good men to come to the aid of their country.*

Amazing, isn't it, the difference one little adjustment can make? A slight turn of the bass or treble knob on my car radio can greatly improve my enjoyment of music. A tad too much sugar absolutely ruins my tea. Once I heard that a fellow student had said she didn't like me, so I decided I didn't like her either. When I changed my thinking and decided to try to win her over, she became a good friend. When I adjust my schedule to allow even fifteen minutes with God in the morning, I have greater peace and joy in my heart the whole day.

You might want to try it today. A slight change in attitude toward a co-worker? A small schedule adjustment to visit a shut-in? A kind word when you normally would hold back? Go ahead—one little thing could make all the difference, in your day…and someone else's.

—Lucile Allen

Prayer Requests

_____

_____

_____

_____

Answered Prayers

_____

_____

_____

_____

God's Touch

_____

_____

_____

_____

26
SUNDAY

"Little by little I will drive them out from before you, until you have increased, and you inherit the land."
—Exodus 23:30

27
MONDAY

"For precept must be upon precept, precept upon precept, line upon line, line upon line, here a little, there a little." —Isaiah 28:10

28
TUESDAY

Better is a little with righteousness, than vast revenues without justice. —Proverbs 16:8

29
WEDNESDAY

But to whom little is forgiven, the same loves little. —Luke 7:47

30
THURSDAY

Even so the tongue is a little member and boasts great things. —James 3:5

31
FRIDAY

Then Jesus said to them, "I shall be with you a little while longer, and then I go to Him who sent Me."
—John 7:33

SEPTEMBER
1
SATURDAY

"He who gathered much had nothing left over, and he who gathered little had no lack." —2 Corinthians 8:15

We spend our days, Lord,
In the places where You plant us.
We thrive and yet we wonder:
What is life like way over there?
Is my neighbor's grass
A little greener?
Until through Your good graces
We see this truth up close:
No matter where we live
We dwell in Your light,
Each of us Your creation …
Remind me, Lord, that I need
Not covet a neighbor's place,
For You are everywhere.

JOY

I've got the joy, joy, joy, joy down in my heart. Down in my heart, down in my heart." The old piano lingered on the last chord as our exuberant voices faded. Every week we sang this Sunday-school chorus, and an unspoken rivalry had risen between the boys and girls to see who could sing loudest. My ten-year-old heart was filled with what I knew must be the joy we were singing about, a tingling that warmed my insides and made my toes wiggle.

Sometimes I feel as though I do, indeed, have the joy "down in my heart," but can't seem to muster it to the surface of my life. I fuss over seams that rip and schedules that conflict. But this month's going to be different. I'm going to remember that the strength to face the tests of life comes not from forced bravado, but from joy. I'm going to trumpet the wonder of stars and wiggle my toes at little delights…things like strong coffee and good music and the touch of a loved one's hand.

—Mary Lou Carney

SEPTEMBER 2012

SUNDAY	MONDAY	TUESDAY	WEDNESDAY	THURSDAY	FRIDAY	SATURDAY
						1
2	3	4	5	6	7	8
9	10	11	12	13	14	15
16	17	18	19	20	21	22
23	24	25	26	27	28	29
30						

Notes

AUGUST

S	M	T	W	T	F	S
			1	2	3	4
5	6	7	8	9	10	11
12	13	14	15	16	17	18
19	20	21	22	23	24	25
26	27	28	29	30	31	

OCTOBER

S	M	T	W	T	F	S
	1	2	3	4	5	6
7	8	9	10	11	12	13
14	15	16	17	18	19	20
21	22	23	24	25	26	27
28	29	30	31			

Before my daughter Lindsay and her new baby were discharged from the hospital, her doctor came to check her out. He reviewed some precautions for Lindsay's first week at home, then sat on the edge of her bed and gave her one last piece of advice.

"Let your husband take care of the baby—and let him do it his way," he said. "If you always tell him how to change her or dress her or burp her, he'll simply stop helping. Babies adjust. And in most cases, the difference doesn't really matter."

Lindsay nodded, probably not yet understanding the wisdom of his words. I nodded knowingly. After all, my husband Lynn and I have been married for thirty-seven years.

A few days later I was watching Lynn cut a cantaloupe in half—the wrong way. Everyone knows you cut a cantaloupe the short way, like a lemon, not end to end. I told him so.

He paused, looking at the cantaloupe. "Why does it matter?" That's when I remembered the doctor's advice. The challenge to accept each other's differences remains the same through all the seasons of marriage.

—Carol Kuykendall

Prayer Requests

Answered Prayers

God's Touch

2
SUNDAY

"I, wisdom, live together with good judgment. I know where to discover knowledge and discernment."
—Proverbs 8:12 (NLT)

3
MONDAY

"I have filled him with the Spirit of God, in wisdom, in understanding, in knowledge, and in all manner of workmanship." —Exodus 31:3
LABOR DAY

4
TUESDAY

My mouth shall speak wisdom, and the meditation of my heart shall give understanding. —Psalm 49:3

5
WEDNESDAY

God gave Solomon wisdom and exceedingly great understanding, and largeness of heart like the sand on the seashore. —1 Kings 4:29

6
THURSDAY

My speech and my preaching were not with persuasive words of human wisdom, but in demonstration of the Spirit and of power. —1 Corinthians 2:4

7
FRIDAY

"If you are wise, your wisdom will reward you...." —Proverbs 9:12

8
SATURDAY

Who is wise and understanding among you? Let him show by good conduct that his works are done in the meekness of wisdom. —James 3:13

Let your light so shine before men, that they may see your good works and glorify your Father in heaven. —MATTHEW 5:6

Tony works behind the counter in one of our neighborhood luncheonettes. I usually say hello when I order my morning coffee, but he never does anything but grunt. So after a while I gave up and ignored him, placing my order with one of the other employees.

But I felt bad about giving Tony the cold shoulder. It seemed clear to me that God wants us to be neighborly toward everyone, whether we like them or not. So one day I gathered up my courage, went over to Tony and said, "Good morning."

No response.

"How's it going?"

Grunt.

"You know, Tony, you make great coffee."

Grunt.

So I decided to go for broke.

"In fact, you make the best coffee in town. If it weren't for you, I'd switch to tea."

That did the trick. Tony turned to me, laughing, and said thanks. It didn't cost me anything, and I earned not only that smile but also a friendly nod every time I go into the café.

Tony is still grumpy and we still don't talk much. But something's opened between us—a chink for God's light to shine through.

—Philip Zaleski

Prayer Requests _____
_____
_____

Answered Prayers _____
_____

God's Touch _____
_____

9
SUNDAY

Therefore let us cast off the works of darkness, and let us put on the armor of light. —Romans 13:12

10
MONDAY

Light is sown for the righteous, and gladness for the upright in heart. —Psalm 97:11

11
TUESDAY

For it is the God who commanded light to shine out of darkness. —2 Corinthians 4:6

12
WEDNESDAY

Then I saw that wisdom excels folly as light excels darkness. —Ecclesiastes 2:13

13
THURSDAY

For You will light my lamp; the Lord my God will enlighten my darkness. —Psalm 18:28

14
FRIDAY

He who says he is in the light, and hates his brother, is in darkness until now. —1 John 2:9

15
SATURDAY

The light of the eyes rejoices the heart, and a good report makes the bones healthy. —Proverbs 15:30

Those who wait on the Lord shall renew their strength;
they shall mount up with wings like eagles. —ISAIAH 40:31

Have you ever noticed how much press is given to the virtue of early rising?

Maybe the writer of Proverbs started it all with words such as "How long wilt thou sleep, O sluggard?" (Proverbs 6:9). But others quickly jumped on the bandwagon with "Early to bed and early to rise makes one healthy, wealthy and wise." Or "The early bird gets the worm." I have a sweatshirt that proclaims, "She who hoots with the owls at night cannot soar with the eagles in the morning."

My sweatshirt was meant to encourage eaglelike habits. But honestly, I'd much rather hoot with the owls. Not that I get to hoot very often. I get up at six o'clock sharp every weekday morning, so I can get to work on time, but I'd prefer later hours.

Recently, however, I read something that improved my attitude toward getting up early. Father Edward Hays wrote, "May my rising be a rehearsal for my resurrection from the dead. With gratitude for the wonder of this day, I enter into silent prayer."

Whether you're an owl or an eagle, rise with gratitude for the blessings God gives us each day.

—Penney Schwab

Prayer Requests _____

_____

_____

_____

Answered Prayers _____

_____

_____

_____

God's Touch _____

_____

_____

_____

16 SUNDAY

At midnight I will rise to give thanks to You, because of Your righteous judgments. —Psalm 119:62

17 MONDAY

Therefore He says: "Awake, you who sleep, Arise from the dead, And Christ will give you light." —Ephesians 5:14
ROSH HASHANAH

18 TUESDAY

Who satisfies your mouth with good things, so that your youth is renewed like the eagle's. —Psalm 103:5

19 WEDNESDAY

Arise, shine; for your light has come! And the glory of the Lord is risen upon you. —Isaiah 60:1

20 THURSDAY

"But you, go your way till the end; for you shall rest, and will arise to your inheritance at the end of the days." —Daniel 12:13

21 FRIDAY

Rise up and help us; rescue us because of your unfailing love. —Psalm 44:26 (NIV)

22 SATURDAY

He guarded him as the apple of his eye, like an eagle that stirs up its nest and hovers over its young. —Deuteronomy 32:10–11 (NIV)
FALL BEGINS

always thought this Scripture meant that it was my job to make sure reconciliation happened before I could be worthy to worship. But what to do when I didn't feel reconciled to a person after confessing my sins against him or her?

"I don't think Jesus wants us to force a reconciliation," a friend suggested, "but instead to try to give the injured person his or her dignity back."

"How?"

"Well," my friend said, "when someone hurts me, 1 feel awful, like I've been devalued, my dignity as a human being discounted. So when I've hurt someone, 1 say something like, '1 can imagine how much what 1 did must have hurt and embarrassed you, and 1 feel sad about doing that. I'm sorry.'"

1 wondered where my friend got the idea to console people instead of trying to get them to forgive you.

"The prayer of St. Francis," my friend revealed. "Help me to seek not so much to be consoled as to console, to be understood as to understand, to be loved as to love."

—Keith Miller

Prayer Requests _____
_____
_____
_____
_____

Answered Prayers _____
_____
_____
_____
_____

God's Touch _____
_____
_____
_____
_____

23
SUNDAY

Now all things are of God, who has reconciled us to Himself through Jesus Christ, and has given us the ministry of reconciliation. —2 Corinthians 5:18

24
MONDAY

He shall pray to God, and He will delight in him, he shall see His face with joy, for He restores to man His righteousness. —Job 33:26

25
TUESDAY

Brethren, if a man is overtaken in any trespass, you who are spiritual restore such a one in a spirit of gentleness. —Galatians 6:1

26
WEDNESDAY

He who covers his sins will not prosper, but whoever confesses and forsakes them will have mercy. —Proverbs 28:13
YOM KIPPUR

27
THURSDAY

"Forgive us our sins, for we also forgive everyone who is indebted to us." —Luke 11:4

28
FRIDAY

"Blessed are those whose lawless deeds are forgiven, and whose sins are covered." —Romans 4:7

29
SATURDAY

For if when we were enemies we were reconciled to God through the death of His Son, much more, having been reconciled, we shall be saved by His life. —Romans 5:10

Dear God,
As the year's end nears
And nights are cold,
We think about things
That warm us—
Like the quilts,
Each one made
Of many pieces—
Different colors, sizes, shapes—
All stitched together
To form a thing of service
And beauty.
Oh, Lord,
Let us not forget
That we, too, come
In varied colors, shapes and sizes,
And by Your grand design
We, too, gain strength
And beauty
From this variety.
Thank You, Lord,
For all our differences.

CURIOSITY

My niece watched me make popcorn and asked, "How's it do that? Explode into popcorn?" I was surprised to realize I didn't know. We went to the encyclopedia and pulled out the "P" voume and read to her about the wonders of popcorn. The evening passed quickly—her questions amazing and humbling me. What happened to my own sense of curiosity? Had I become so used to the wonders of light switches and color photographs and purple sunsets that I no longer paused to ponder these marvels?

This month, as autumn begins to take center stage, I'm going to wonder. About colored leaves and frosty window panes. I'm going to read, take a trip to the museum, talk to my mechanic. I'm going to see with the eyes of a child those everyday phenomena—and people—I sometimes take for granted.

—Mary Lou Carney

OCTOBER 2012

SUNDAY	MONDAY	TUESDAY	WEDNESDAY	THURSDAY	FRIDAY	SATURDAY
	1	2	3	4	5	6
7	8	9	10	11	12	13
14	15	16	17	18	19	20
21	22	23	24	25	26	27
28	29	30	31			

Notes

SEPTEMBER

S	M	T	W	T	F	S
						1
2	3	4	5	6	7	8
9	10	11	12	13	14	15
16	17	18	19	20	21	22
23/30	24	25	26	27	28	29

NOVEMBER

S	M	T	W	T	F	S
				1	2	3
4	5	6	7	8	9	10
11	12	13	14	15	16	17
18	19	20	21	22	23	24
25	26	27	28	29	30	

Let a man so consider us, as servants of Christ
and stewards of the mysteries of God. —1 CORINTHIANS 4:1

*B*rad, doesn't this bathroom smell awesome?" I exclaimed. It had just been cleaned and they'd used something that smelled good, which was unusual.

My friend from the third floor of my college dormitory looked at me, perhaps wondering what kind of person would get excited about the olfactory elements of a public restroom.

"Actually," he said, "I have no sense of smell."

"What?" I asked in disbelief.

"Yeah, I was born that way."

I was at a loss for words.

"Weird."

He smiled.

"So what's it smell like in here?"

"Pineapples."

"Oh…well, what do pineapples smell like?"

How do you describe scent to someone who has never smelled? It's simply impossible. How could I help him imagine the smells of Thanksgiving dinner, an ocean breeze or even a clean bathroom? It would be like trying to explain how God has always existed, or how our souls will live forever, or how an invisible Spirit can dwell in a physical being. Some things are mysteries, impossible to explain.

"It's fresh," I began, "like a spring rain." For a friend I could try.

—Joshua Sundquist

Prayer Requests _____

_____

Answered Prayers _____

_____

God's Touch _____

_____

30

SUNDAY

"Can you fathom the mysteries of God? Can you probe the limits of the Almighty?" —Job 11:7 (NIV)

OCTOBER

1

MONDAY

Truly, O God of Israel, our Savior, you work in mysterious ways. —Isaiah 45:15 (NLT)

2

TUESDAY

Pray also for me, that whenever I speak, words may be given me so that I will fearlessly make known the mystery of the gospel, —Ephesians 6:19 (NIV)

3

WEDNESDAY

"For with God nothing will be impossible." —Luke 1:37

4

THURSDAY

We speak the wisdom of God in a mystery, the hidden wisdom which God ordained before the ages for our glory. —1 Corinthians 2:7

5

FRIDAY

Solomon had answers for all her questions; nothing was too hard for him to explain to her. —2 Chronicles 9:2

6

SATURDAY

Oh, the depth of the riches both of the wisdom and knowledge of God! How unsearchable are His judgments and His ways past finding out! —Romans 11:33

And when we cried unto the Lord, He heard our voice,
and sent an angel.... —NUMBERS 20:16 (KJV)

When I was young, I was enchanted by angels: Michael with his flaming sword…pastel-winged Gabriel…my guardian angel…heavenly hosts. Everywhere I went I listened expectantly, and sometimes I even heard the rustle of wings.

Then I grew up. I forgot all about angels—until one day…I was expecting a beloved friend to visit. Somehow, I hadn't noticed that the hedge had become a forest and the lawn was a full-fledged meadow. Ruefully I sighed, "Well, I can cook, Lord, but I'll have to leave the gardening to You."

That afternoon a courteous youth and his father appeared at my door. They were looking for a yard to "do." And they "did" mine—to perfection. I took their phone number and later called it, hoping to thank them. There was no answer.

"Well," I surprised myself by thinking, "maybe angels don't answer phones!" And I never saw or heard from the pair again.

Now I try to be more expectant, watching for the "angels" who pass through my daily life. And I'm content to accept them as such with a heart full of thanksgiving.

—Elaine St. Johns

Prayer Requests _____
_____
_____
_____

Answered Prayers _____
_____
_____
_____

God's Touch _____
_____
_____
_____

For He shall give His angels charge over you, to keep you in all your ways. —Psalm 91:11

7
SUNDAY

And the Angel of the Lord appeared to him, and said to him, "The Lord is with you, you mighty man of valor!" —Judges 6:12

COLUMBUS DAY

8
MONDAY

Then an angel appeared to Him from heaven, strengthening Him. —Luke 22:43

9
TUESDAY

"For there stood by me this night an angel of the God to whom I belong and whom I serve, saying, 'Do not be afraid....'" —Acts 27:23, 24

10
WEDNESDAY

"Behold, I send an Angel before you to keep you in the way and to bring you into the place which I have prepared." —Exodus 23:20

11
THURSDAY

And she saw two angels in white sitting, one at the head and the other at the feet, where the body of Jesus had lain. —John 20:12

12
FRIDAY

Do not forget to entertain strangers, for by so doing some have unwittingly entertained angels. —Hebrews 13:2

13
SATURDAY

As a magazine editor I interview fascinating and inspirational people. I'll never forget the first time I met with Jim Stoval and his wife, Crystal, in New York City. As Crystal and I talked at a restaurant table, Jim entered the crowded room, navigated his way around, reached our table, and held out his hand. Later he asked the waiter if it would be all right for him to play the grand piano he'd passed and then sat down and played a medley of show tunes to the delight of diners and staff. Jim is one of the most positive, focused and energetic people I've ever met. He's also blind.

In his twenties Jim was diagnosed with a degenerative eye disease.

Instead of retreating into isolation and self-pity, he became a highly successful businessman, speaker and author.

"How do you do it?" I asked him. "How do you go out into the world, all over the world, and face the unknown each day?"

Jim responded with a deep, rolling laugh. "Mary Ann," he said in his Oklahoma baritone, "that's why the prayer says, 'Give us *this* day our daily bread.'"

—Mary Ann O'Roark

Prayer Requests _____

_____

_____

_____

Answered Prayers _____

_____

_____

_____

God's Touch _____

_____

_____

_____

14
SUNDAY

Blessed is the man who listens to me [wisdom], watching daily at my gates, waiting at the posts of my doors. —Proverbs 8:34

15
MONDAY

Acknowledge and take to heart this day that the Lord is God in heaven above and on the earth below. There is no other. —Deuteronomy 4:39 (NIV)

16
TUESDAY

Also Jehoshaphat said to the king of Israel, "Please inquire for the word of the Lord today." —1 Kings 22:5

17
WEDNESDAY

"Today, if you will hear His voice, do not harden your hearts." —Hebrews 4:7

18
THURSDAY

Then He said to them all, "If anyone desires to come after Me, let him deny himself, and take up his cross daily, and follow Me." —Luke 9:23

19
FRIDAY

Continuing daily with one accord in the temple, and breaking bread from house to house, they ate their food with gladness and simplicity of heart. —Acts 2:46

20
SATURDAY

Blessed be the Lord, Who daily loads us with benefits, the God of our salvation! —Psalm 68:19

My mother had many virtues, but she had one persistent if amusing fault. She took the weather personally. A beautiful day she regarded almost as her individual benediction. She sang and accomplished things and loved the world. On gloomy days, she would stew and fuss.

My grandfather, on the other hand, had two dear homilies that he applied to life's situations, including the weather: "It's all for the best, but we can't see it" and "No great damage without some small good." When hailstones battered the crops, or droughts parched the fields, or a cyclone took the roof off the barn, "We'll be strengthened by this adversity," he'd solemnly declare. "The barn needs a new roof anyway, and look how many neighbors want to help. Why, except for this we'd never appreciate how good people are."

Grandpa's philosophy has helped me through many of life's storms.

—Marjorie Holmes

Prayer Requests _____

_____

_____

_____

Answered Prayers _____

_____

_____

_____

God's Touch _____

_____

_____

_____

21
SUNDAY

"Shall we indeed accept good from God, and shall we not accept adversity?" —Job 2:10

22
MONDAY

Trouble pursues the sinner, but the righteous are rewarded with good things. —Proverbs 13:21

23
TUESDAY

In the day of prosperity be joyful, but in the day of adversity consider: Surely God has appointed the one as well as the other. —Ecclesiastes 7:14

24
WEDNESDAY

This poor man cried out, and the Lord heard him, and saved him out of all his troubles. —Psalm 34:6
UNITED NATIONS DAY

25
THURSDAY

Though the Lord gave you adversity for food and suffering for drink, he will still be with you to teach you. —Isaiah 30:20 (NLT)

26
FRIDAY

But God was with him and delivered him out of all his troubles. —Acts 7:9–10

27
SATURDAY

A friend loves at all times, and a brother is born for adversity. —Proverbs 17:17

Bring all the tithes into the storehouse.... —MALACHI 3:10

I look forward to seeing my sister's family for many reasons, not the least of which are the lessons on God's love that Max, my nephew, is sure to teach me.

I had confessed to Max's father, Tedd, that I struggle with the concept of tithing. "I know that we're called to be cheerful givers," I said, "but it often seemed like a choice—tithe or help my son with his college expenses."

Tedd told me that he and Becky had gone through the same struggle. They just didn't see how they could be generous to God and still provide for their children. What they didn't know was that Max, playing nearby, had overheard part of their conversation.

"What's a tithe?" he asked his father as he skipped into the room.

When Tedd explained the concept of giving ten percent of our money to God, Max was amazed. "Wow!" he said. "You mean that God lets us keep ninety percent of everything?" Then he raced away to resume his play.

Max had it right: A tithe is an example of God's generosity, not ours.

—Tim Williams

Prayer Requests _____

_____

_____

_____

Answered Prayers _____

_____

_____

_____

God's Touch _____

_____

_____

_____

28 SUNDAY	But a generous man devises generous things, and by generosity he shall stand. —Isaiah 32:8
29 MONDAY	Command them to do good, to be rich in good deeds, and to be generous and willing to share. —1 Timothy 6:18 (NIV)
30 TUESDAY	The generous soul will be made rich, and he who waters will also be watered himself. —Proverbs 11:25
31 WEDNESDAY	"Don't I have the right to do what I want with my own money? Or are you envious because I am generous?" —Matthew 20:15 (NIV) HALLOWEEN
NOVEMBER **1** THURSDAY	Restore to me the joy of Your salvation, and uphold me by Your generous Spirit. —Psalm 51:12 ALL SAINTS' DAY
2 FRIDAY	Good will come to those who are generous and lend freely, who conduct their affairs with justice. —Psalm 112:5 (NIV)
3 SATURDAY	You will be enriched in every way so that you can be generous on every occasion, and through us your generosity will result in thanksgiving to God. —2 Corinthians 9:11 (NIV)

Dear Lord,
There are those who have little,
And those who give much.
Dear God,
This Thanksgiving
We too want to show our
Thanks
By giving.
Help us to work with
Our own loaves and fishes
Our own talents and
Compassion —
To "feed" others.
For it's true that,
When you're doing the
Lord's work,
Things begin to multiply
In amazing ways.

ADVENTURE

*A*nd you know what happened then?" The first-graders leaned forward, captivated by my Pilgrim costume and my first-person account of Thanksgiving. "Dozens of Indians came out of the forest...." After the story, one little girl commented, "That was some adventure you Pilgrims had!" I nodded assent. "I had an adventure last night!" she added.

"Really? Tell me about it."

"Me and my little sister walked to the dry cleaners all by ourselves. Past this yappy dog on our block. We have adventures all the time. Last week we made brownies."

Driving home, I thought about what new "adventures" I had experienced lately. Everything in my life seemed so routine. Why risk taking that class if I might fail? How did I know the new family on the block wanted someone to visit them? I knew the truth. I was afraid to take risks, afraid to have "adventures." I was dependent on what I knew.

This month, let's be adventurous—try a new restaurant, or a new recipe. Join a book group, a neighborhood coffee club. Let's live each day courageously, knowing that our source of help is sure.

—Mary Lou Carney

NOVEMBER 2012

SUNDAY	MONDAY	TUESDAY	WEDNESDAY	THURSDAY	FRIDAY	SATURDAY
				1	2	3
4	5	6	7	8	9	10
11	12	13	14	15	16	17
18	19	20	21	22	23	24
25	26	27	28	29	30	

Notes

OCTOBER

S	M	T	W	T	F	S
	1	2	3	4	5	6
7	8	9	10	11	12	13
14	15	16	17	18	19	20
21	22	23	24	25	26	27
28	29	30	31			

DECEMBER

S	M	T	W	T	F	S
						1
2	3	4	5	6	7	8
9	10	11	12	13	14	15
16	17	18	19	20	21	22
23/30	24/31	25	26	27	28	29

> *There is no authority except from God, and the authorities that exist are appointed by God.* —ROMANS 13:1

Election year is a terrible time to live in Washington, DC. Everyone gets caught up in politics, and often the rhetoric gets downright ugly.

My wife, Joy, and I serve as volunteers for the National Prayer Breakfast, which is a completely nonpartisan event. Like the military, our group is supposed to respect and serve to the best of our ability whoever is elected president. Often that's not easy.

On the Thursday before the last national election, some prayer-breakfast volunteers were at lunch together. Everything was fine until someone mentioned a story from that morning's newspaper. Suddenly, battle lines were drawn and tempers started to rise.

Rapping his spoon loudly on the table, the senior member of the group got everyone's attention. "Look," he said, "everyone calm down. There are two things we know for sure about the election. First, after all the uproar next Tuesday, we'll be back here next Thursday eager to do our best. And second, whoever is elected, God will still be in charge."

—Eric Fellman

Prayer Requests

Answered Prayers

God's Touch

4
SUNDAY

For the kingdom is the Lord's, and He rules over the nations. —Psalm 22:28
DAYLIGHT SAVING TIME ENDS

5
MONDAY

"For I also am a man under authority, having soldiers under me." —Matthew 8:9

6
TUESDAY

He said to him, "Well done, good servant; because you were faithful in a very little, have authority over ten cities." —Luke 19:17
ELECTION DAY

7
WEDNESDAY

"You shall not revile God, nor curse a ruler of your people." —Exodus 22:28

8
THURSDAY

He who is slow to anger is better than the mighty, and he who rules his spirit than he who takes a city. —Proverbs 16:32

9
FRIDAY

"By what authority are You doing these things? And who gave You this authority?" —Matthew 21:23

10
SATURDAY

When the righteous are in authority, the people rejoice; but when a wicked man rules, the people groan. —Proverbs 29:2

> **Let no corrupt word proceed out of your mouth,
> but what is good for necessary edification.** —EPHESIANS 4:29

You look fat! You're pathetic. How could you be so stupid?

Wouldn't you cringe if you heard someone talking like that? Well, guess what? That's how lots of us talk to ourselves, and after a while we believe it. I should know. I've been at this bad habit for a long time.

Here's an example: I walk into my closet and go at it. *Those pants are too tight. Your arms look like sausages in that sweater. Why can't you lose weight?* By the time I'm dressed, I don't like myself.

My friend Kathy understands, because we often commiserate over our weaknesses. But Kathy's a counselor, so she's one step ahead of me. "When you catch yourself talking like that, stop!" she said. "Then talk to yourself like you'd talk to a friend. Me, for instance."

Okay, so I'm back in the closet. *Not that skirt! You can't even zip it up….*

Stop! If Kathy were here in my shoes, how would I help her decide what to wear? "What would be fun—and make you feel good today? You look good in this…."

Get the picture?

—Carol Kuykendall

Prayer Requests _____

_____

_____

Answered Prayers _____

_____

_____

_____

God's Touch _____

_____

_____

11
SUNDAY

All things are lawful for me, but not all things are helpful; all things are lawful for me, but not all things edify.
—1 Corinthians 10:23
VETERANS DAY

12
MONDAY

Your words have supported those who were falling; you encouraged those with shaky knees. —Job 4:4 (NLT)

13
TUESDAY

My tongue shall speak of Your word, for all Your commandments are righteousness. —Psalm 119:172

14
WEDNESDAY

The metalworker encourages the goldsmith, and the one who smooths with the hammer spurs on the one who strikes the anvil. —Isaiah 41:7 (NIV)

15
THURSDAY

I weep with sorrow; encourage me by your word. —Psalm 119:28 (NLT)

16
FRIDAY

Therefore comfort each other and edify one another, just as you also are doing. —1 Thessalonians 5:11

17
SATURDAY

Therefore let us pursue the things which make for peace and the things by which one may edify another.
—Romans 14:19

One day I found myself in a grouchy mood. I inflicted my grumbling on family and friends until someone challenged me to spend one full day giving thanks to God for *everything*.

It should be easy to give God thanks, I thought. *Just do it!*

The next morning I started down for coffee. But what was that all over the walls? Swirling…writhing…

Tiny insects—thousands of them. The front door had been left open a crack and the bugs swarmed in. For two hours my wife Tib and I shooed, swatted, vacuumed until the last bug vanished. But so had my morning. I said a shallow, "Thank You, God."

And that was just the beginning. The car battery was dead: *Thank You, God.* A story disappeared into the innards of my computer: *Thank You.* Tib got stuck in a traffic tie-up and missed the doctor's appointment she'd waited months for. *Thank You, God.*

As the day went on, I found I was immersed in an atmosphere of thanksgiving that was beginning— just beginning—to be independent of circumstances.

Thanksgiving takes us beyond the circumstances to the Father Who stands beside us in the circumstances.

—John Sherrill

Prayer Requests

_____
_____
_____

Answered Prayers

_____
_____
_____
_____

God's Touch

_____
_____
_____

18
SUNDAY

"I thank You and praise You, O God of my fathers; You have given me wisdom and might…." —Daniel 2:23

19
MONDAY

Then I will thank you in front of the great assembly. I will praise you before all the people. —Psalm 35:18 (NLT)

20
TUESDAY

And Jesus lifted up His eyes and said, "Father, I thank You that You have heard Me." —John 11:41

21
WEDNESDAY

I thank you for answering my prayer and giving me victory! —Psalm 118:21 (NLT)

22
THURSDAY

"Now therefore, our God, we thank You And praise Your glorious name." —1 Chronicles 29:13
THANKSGIVING

23
FRIDAY

In everything give thanks; for this is the will of God in Christ Jesus for you. —1 Thessalonians 5:18

24
SATURDAY

So we, Your people and sheep of Your pasture, will give You thanks forever; we will show forth Your praise to all generations. —Psalm 79:13

*"For the bread of God is he who comes down
from heaven and gives life to the world."* —JOHN 6:33

I had to be out on an errand early. I overslept a bit and didn't have time for breakfast, so when I returned to the house, I automatically hurried to the kitchen for a cup of tea and a muffin.

Upstairs a pile of unanswered letters, a mound of laundry, and a half-written manuscript awaited me. Soon it would be time to pick up the children.

Do I have time to read my Bible? I wondered. I felt so duty bound to the chores of the day.

Then my eye fell on the teacup and the muffin crumbs on the table. On coming in, hadn't my first priority been automatically to feed my body? Then wasn't my next priority to feed my soul? I did just that. I took up my Bible and discovered once again that both bodies and souls function best when they've been nourished!

—Patricia Houck Sprinkle

Prayer Requests _____

_____

_____

_____

_____

Answered Prayers _____

_____

_____

_____

_____

God's Touch _____

_____

_____

_____

_____

25
SUNDAY

"As the living Father sent Me, and I live because of the Father, so he who feeds on Me will live because of Me."
—John 6:57

26
MONDAY

Trust in the Lord, and do good; dwell in the land, and feed on His faithfulness. —Psalm 37:3

27
TUESDAY

Jesus answered him, saying, "It is written, 'Man shall not live by bread alone, but by every word of God.'"
—Luke 4:4

28
WEDNESDAY

They continued steadfastly in the apostles' doctrine and fellowship, in the breaking of bread, and in prayers.
—Acts 2:42

29
THURSDAY

He…had rained down manna on them to eat, and given them of the bread of heaven. —Psalm 78:24

30
FRIDAY

I have not departed from the commandment of His lips; I have treasured the words of His mouth more than my necessary food. —Job 23:12

DECEMBER
1
SATURDAY

All ate the same spiritual food, and all drank the same spiritual drink. For they drank of that spiritual Rock that followed them, and that Rock was Christ. —1 Corinthians 10:3, 4

Heavenly Father,
We can see
The progress of
Mary and Joseph
As they journeyed
Toward the most
Blessed Event
In the history
Of the world.
Now, as once more
We approach the day
Of Your Son's birth,
Help us feel the
Holiness of this
Time. Help us honor
The spirit of
Your wondrous gift
To us in Bethlehem:
Love.

HOPE

*M*y sister explained why she couldn't tell what she wished for: "If you tell, it won't come true. The power of wishes is in the wanting and waiting, not in the telling!"

What wonderful wishes those birthday ones were! Show ponies and shiny bicycles. Seldom did any of these dreams materialize exactly the way we planned, but our spirits were undaunted. There was always next year's birthday cake—with even more candles to wish on!

But hope is more difficult in the adult world. I find myself impatient when my prayers aren't answered quickly or exactly as I wanted. I become trapped in concrete realities that frustrate and paralyze me. I forget the power of wanting and waiting.

What better time than Advent to stretch toward unseen realities that await us, to truly believe in the substance of the invisible? I'm going to hope—for family health and safe trips. For a chance to help someone. For parking spots. For a white Christmas. For world peace.

—Mary Lou Carney

DECEMBER 2012

SUNDAY	MONDAY	TUESDAY	WEDNESDAY	THURSDAY	FRIDAY	SATURDAY
						1
2	3	4	5	6	7	8
9	10	11	12	13	14	15
16	17	18	19	20	21	22
23 / 30	24 / 31	25	26	27	28	29

Notes

NOVEMBER

S	M	T	W	T	F	S
				1	2	3
4	5	6	7	8	9	10
11	12	13	14	15	16	17
18	19	20	21	22	23	24
25	26	27	28	29	30	

JANUARY

S	M	T	W	T	F	S
		1	2	3	4	5
6	7	8	9	10	11	12
13	14	15	16	17	18	19
20	21	22	23	24	25	26
27	28	29	30	31		

GUIDEPOSTS DAILY PLANNER

He performs wonders that cannot be fathomed,
miracles that cannot be counted. —JOB 5:9 (NIV)

I taught a children's Sunday-school class for several years. Because our congregation was small, all the children came to my class. I'd been wondering if I should turn the class over to someone younger.

Then one Sunday I took a brown paper bag to Sunday school and held it up for the children to see.

"I've got one of God's great miracles inside this bag," I said.

When I pulled out a big red apple, one child asked skeptically, "That's a miracle?"

"Yes, I said. "Just watch."

I cut the core out of the apple and extracted eight black seeds. "Each seed contains an apple tree," I explained.

"No way," another child said.

"Yes, way," I said. "Eight seeds, eight trees inside this one apple. And each of those eight trees has the ability to grow thousands of apples during its lifetime."

"Wow!" exclaimed a third child. "That *is* a miracle!"

When the children left the class that day, one of them said, "You're a good teacher."

I decided to hang in there a little longer.

—Madge Harrah

Prayer Requests _____

_____

_____

_____

Answered Prayers _____

_____

_____

_____

God's Touch _____

_____

_____

_____

2
SUNDAY

God has appointed these in the church: first apostles, second prophets, third teachers, after that miracles....
—1 Corinthians 12:28
FIRST SUNDAY IN ADVENT

3
MONDAY

I will remember the deeds of the Lord; yes, I will remember your miracles of long ago. —Psalm 77:11 (NIV)

4
TUESDAY

The multitudes with one accord heeded the things spoken by Philip, hearing and seeing the miracles which he did. —Acts 8:6

5
WEDNESDAY

And he did not do many miracles there because of their lack of faith. —Matthew 13:58 (NIV)

6
THURSDAY

You are the God who performs miracles; you display your power among the peoples. —Psalm 77:14 (NIV)

7
FRIDAY

Now God worked unusual miracles by the hands of Paul. —Acts 19:11

8
SATURDAY

"When Pharaoh says to you, 'Perform a miracle,' then say to Aaron, 'Take your staff and throw it down before Pharaoh,' and it will become a snake." —Exodus 7:9 (NIV)

I noticed them as I drove home that dark evening. Someone had wrapped strings of lights around all the tree trunks in his front yard. Round and round the twinkling colors went, but only about six feet up. After that, the trees ascended heavenward in darkness. *Odd*, I thought. But the next night, as I approached the lights, they didn't seem so odd. They seemed, well, pragmatic.

I had no idea why the lights stopped so abruptly. Perhaps the homeowner didn't have a ladder or wasn't permitted to climb for some reason. Perhaps he had a limited number of lights and a limited budget. Perhaps he didn't have much time for decorating but wanted to make the effort. Whatever his reason for this unusual display, it inspired me. He had done what he could with what he had.

Kind of like Mary and Joseph in the stable, with a manger for a crib and beds made of fresh straw. Perhaps that's all God ever requires of us: to do the best we can with what we have. It was a comforting thought to ponder while driving through December darkness.

—Mary Lou Carney

Prayer Requests _____
_____
_____
_____
_____

Answered Prayers _____
_____
_____
_____
_____

God's Touch _____
_____
_____
_____
_____

9
SUNDAY

Do your best to present yourself to God as one approved, a worker who does not need to be ashamed and who correctly handles the word of truth. —2 Timothy 2:15 (NIV)
SECOND SUNDAY IN ADVENT / HANUKKAH

10
MONDAY

The Lord says, "I will guide you along the best pathway for your life. I will advise you and watch over you." —Psalm 32:8 (NLT)

11
TUESDAY

"Bring your father and your households and come to me; I will give you the best of the land of Egypt, and you will eat the fat of the land." —Genesis 45:18

12
WEDNESDAY

"But the father said to his servants, 'Bring out the best robe and put it on him, and put a ring on his hand and sandals on his feet.'" —Luke 15:22

13
THURSDAY

"All the best of the oil, all the best of the new wine and the grain, their firstfruits which they offer to the Lord, I have given them to you." —Numbers 18:12

14
FRIDAY

So you should earnestly desire the most helpful gifts. But now let me show you a way of life that is best of all. —1 Corinthians 12:31 (NLT)

15
SATURDAY

Each time he said, "My grace is all you need. My power works best in weakness." —2 Corinthians 12:9 (NLT)

How are you doing?" my pastor Peter gently asked my husband, Lynn, and me as we sat around our dinner table.

I hardly knew how to answer that since Lynn and I had both been diagnosed with cancer. After an update about our recent chemotherapy treatments, I confessed something that had been troubling me.

"I've let my world grow very small," I said. "I have good reason to hide here at home. I don't feel so good. My immune system is down. I feel self-conscious wearing a wig."

Peter paused. "This may not make sense to you, but people need to see you. You encourage them when you just show up. It's a…ministry of presence."

The next Sunday Lynn and I went to church. The following week, I got several notes.

"It gave me hope to see you in church on Sunday."

"Seeing you face your battle helps me know I can face mine."

The ministry of presence is about showing up so God can use my presence for His purposes in the lives of others—at church, at a social gathering, maybe even at the grocery store.

—Carol Kuykendall

Prayer Requests _____

_____

_____

_____

Answered Prayers _____

_____

_____

_____

God's Touch _____

_____

_____

_____

16
SUNDAY

The Lord replied, "My Presence will go with you, and I will give you rest." —Exodus 33:14 (NIV)
THIRD SUNDAY IN ADVENT

17
MONDAY

And truly Jesus did many other signs in the presence of His disciples, which are not written in this book.
—John 20:30

18
TUESDAY

You prepare a table before me in the presence of my enemies; You anoint my head with oil; my cup runs over.
—Psalm 23:5

19
WEDNESDAY

For what is our hope, or joy, or crown of rejoicing? Is it not even you in the presence of our Lord Jesus Christ at His coming? —1 Thessalonians 2:19

20
THURSDAY

"Likewise, I say to you, there is joy in the presence of the angels of God over one sinner who repents."
—Luke 15:10

21
FRIDAY

So they departed from the presence of the council, rejoicing that they were counted worthy to suffer shame for His name. —Acts 5:41
WINTER BEGINS

22
SATURDAY

Fight the good fight of faith, lay hold on eternal life, to which you were also called and have confessed the good confession in the presence of many witnesses. —1 Timothy 6:12

I knew it was a mistake to go to Walmart on a Saturday two weeks before Christmas! Carts choked the aisles, the picture frames were at the opposite end of the vast floor from men's sweaters, and the store-brand lights were incompatible with our old set.

At the checkout, the shortest line had ten people. The weary young cashier swiped the bar codes and bagged the purchases without ever glancing at the customer.

I pushed my cart out to the lot. As I lifted bags into the trunk, a woman was loading her own car nearby. A little farther off, a man was doing the same—apparently her husband because he called to ask if she had the Santa lawn ornament. The woman got into her car.

"Love you!" she called as she shut the door.

Two words ringing out in a crowded parking lot. *Love you.* That's what the jammed aisles, the laden carts, the lines were all about. All of us had come that day on our personal errands of love. And love is always costly. Love demands time, resources, energy. It requires a lifetime of giving.

—Elizabeth Sherrill

Prayer Requests _____

_____

_____

Answered Prayers _____

_____

_____

God's Touch _____

_____

_____

23 SUNDAY

Though I bestow all my goods to feed the poor, and though I give my body to be burned, but have not love, it profits me nothing. —1 Corinthians 13:3

FOURTH SUNDAY IN ADVENT

24 MONDAY

The Father loves the Son, and has given all things into His hand. —John 3:35

CHRISTMAS EVE

25 TUESDAY

So let each one give as he purposes in his heart, not grudgingly or of necessity; for God loves a cheerful giver. —2 Corinthians 9:7

CHRISTMAS

26 WEDNESDAY

"You shall love your neighbor as yourself." —Mark 12:31

27 THURSDAY

For this is the message that you heard from the beginning, that we should love one another. —1 John 3:11

28 FRIDAY

"A new commandment I give to you, that you love one another; as I have loved you, that you also love one another." —John 13:34

29 SATURDAY

"Eye has not seen, nor ear heard, nor have entered into the heart of man the things which God has prepared for those who love Him." —1 Corinthians 2:9

> *"For behold, I create new heavens and a new earth; and the former shall not be remembered or come to mind."* —ISAIAH 65:17

When my wife, Shirley, and I are in Florida, we go out our back door every evening and watch the sun set over the Gulf of Mexico. Our neighbors know all about my sunset rating system—ten for the most colorful, on down to one. Tonight's was about a six, but it was special because it was the last day of the year.

As the shadow of years grows longer, I have a tendency to look back on my successes and failures. Tonight, as I studied the sandy shore and the gentle waves that caressed it, I was reminded of Anne Morrow Lindbergh's classic book *The Gift from the Sea*, about the tide erasing everything it touches…all our scribbling, all our footprints. Like lost memories. Sometimes we forget things we'd like to remember, but it's also true that some baggage is best left behind.

That's why this is a good day to accept God's forgiving grace and get on with life. With His help, I can turn away from old sunsets—no matter how beautiful—and look to the redeeming dawn of the new year.

—Fred Bauer

Prayer Requests _____

_____

_____

_____

Answered Prayers _____

_____

_____

_____

God's Touch _____

_____

_____

_____

30
SUNDAY

"Behold, the former things have come to pass, and new things I declare; before they spring forth I tell you of them." —Isaiah 42:9

31
MONDAY

"For this is My blood of the new covenant, which is shed for many for the remission of sins." —Matthew 26:28

NEW YEAR'S EVE

JANUARY 2013
1
TUESDAY

I will give them one heart, and I will put a new spirit within them, and take the stony heart out of their flesh, and give them a heart of flesh. —Ezekiel 11:19

NEW YEAR'S DAY

2
WEDNESDAY

Likewise He also took the cup after supper, saying, "This cup is the new covenant in My blood, which is shed for you." —Luke 22:20

3
THURSDAY

He has put a new song in my mouth—praise to our God. —Psalm 40:3

4
FRIDAY

I have made you hear new things from this time, even hidden things, and you did not know them. —Isaiah 48:6

5
SATURDAY

Oh, sing to the Lord a new song! Sing to the Lord, all the earth. —Psalm 96:1

JANUARY 2013

SUNDAY	MONDAY	TUESDAY	WEDNESDAY	THURSDAY	FRIDAY	SATURDAY
		1	2	3	4	5
6	7	8	9	10	11	12
13	14	15	16	17	18	19
20	21	22	23	24	25	26
27	28	29	30	31		

FEBRUARY 2013

SUNDAY	MONDAY	TUESDAY	WEDNESDAY	THURSDAY	FRIDAY	SATURDAY
					1	2
3	4	5	6	7	8	9
10	11	12	13	14	15	16
17	18	19	20	21	22	23
24	25	26	27	28		

MARCH 2013

SUNDAY	MONDAY	TUESDAY	WEDNESDAY	THURSDAY	FRIDAY	SATURDAY
					1	2
3	4	5	6	7	8	9
10	11	12	13	14	15	16
17	18	19	20	21	22	23
24	25	26	27	28	29	30
31						

APRIL 2013

SUNDAY	MONDAY	TUESDAY	WEDNESDAY	THURSDAY	FRIDAY	SATURDAY
	1	2	3	4	5	6
7	8	9	10	11	12	13
14	15	16	17	18	19	20
21	22	23	24	25	26	27
28	29	30				

2013 CALENDAR

JANUARY						
S	M	T	W	T	F	S
		1	2	3	4	5
6	7	8	9	10	11	12
13	14	15	16	17	18	19
20	21	22	23	24	25	26
27	28	29	30	31		

FEBRUARY						
S	M	T	W	T	F	S
					1	2
3	4	5	6	7	8	9
10	11	12	13	14	15	16
17	18	19	20	21	22	23
24	25	26	27	28		

MARCH						
S	M	T	W	T	F	S
					1	2
3	4	5	6	7	8	9
10	11	12	13	14	15	16
17	18	19	20	21	22	23
24/31	25	26	27	28	29	30

APRIL						
S	M	T	W	T	F	S
	1	2	3	4	5	6
7	8	9	10	11	12	13
14	15	16	17	18	19	20
21	22	23	24	25	26	27
28	29	30				

MAY						
S	M	T	W	T	F	S
			1	2	3	4
5	6	7	8	9	10	11
12	13	14	15	16	17	18
19	20	21	22	23	24	25
26	27	28	29	30	31	

JUNE						
S	M	T	W	T	F	S
						1
2	3	4	5	6	7	8
9	10	11	12	13	14	15
16	17	18	19	20	21	22
23/30	24	25	26	27	28	29

JULY						
S	M	T	W	T	F	S
	1	2	3	4	5	6
7	8	9	10	11	12	13
14	15	16	17	18	19	20
21	22	23	24	25	26	27
28	29	30	31			

AUGUST						
S	M	T	W	T	F	S
				1	2	3
4	5	6	7	8	9	10
11	12	13	14	15	16	17
18	19	20	21	22	23	24
25	26	27	28	29	30	31

SEPTEMBER						
S	M	T	W	T	F	S
1	2	3	4	5	6	7
8	9	10	11	12	13	14
15	16	17	18	19	20	21
22	23	24	25	26	27	28
29	30					

OCTOBER						
S	M	T	W	T	F	S
		1	2	3	4	5
6	7	8	9	10	11	12
13	14	15	16	17	18	19
20	21	22	23	24	25	26
27	28	29	30	31		

NOVEMBER						
S	M	T	W	T	F	S
					1	2
3	4	5	6	7	8	9
10	11	12	13	14	15	16
17	18	19	20	21	22	23
24	25	26	27	28	29	30

DECEMBER						
S	M	T	W	T	F	S
1	2	3	4	5	6	7
8	9	10	11	12	13	14
15	16	17	18	19	20	21
22	23	24	25	26	27	28
29	30	31				

2014 CALENDAR

JANUARY						
S	M	T	W	T	F	S
			1	2	3	4
5	6	7	8	9	10	11
12	13	14	15	16	17	18
19	20	21	22	23	24	25
26	27	28	29	30	31	

FEBRUARY						
S	M	T	W	T	F	S
						1
2	3	4	5	6	7	8
9	10	11	12	13	14	15
16	17	18	19	20	21	22
23	24	25	26	27	28	

MARCH						
S	M	T	W	T	F	S
						1
2	3	4	5	6	7	8
9	10	11	12	13	14	15
16	17	18	19	20	21	22
23/30	24/31	25	26	27	28	29

OCTOBER						
S	M	T	W	T	F	S
			1	2	3	4
5	6	7	8	9	10	11
12	13	14	15	16	17	18
19	20	21	22	23	24	25
26	27	28	29	30	31	

MAY						
S	M	T	W	T	F	S
				1	2	3
4	5	6	7	8	9	10
11	12	13	14	15	16	17
18	19	20	21	22	23	24
25	26	27	28	29	30	31

JUNE						
S	M	T	W	T	F	S
1	2	3	4	5	6	7
8	9	10	11	12	13	14
15	16	17	18	19	20	21
22	23	24	25	26	27	28
29	30					

JULY						
S	M	T	W	T	F	S
		1	2	3	4	5
6	7	8	9	10	11	12
13	14	15	16	17	18	19
20	21	22	23	24	25	26
27	28	29	30	31		

AUGUST						
S	M	T	W	T	F	S
					1	2
3	4	5	6	7	8	9
10	11	12	13	14	15	16
17	18	19	20	21	22	23
24/31	25	26	27	28	29	30

SEPTEMBER						
S	M	T	W	T	F	S
	1	2	3	4	5	6
7	8	9	10	11	12	13
14	15	16	17	18	19	20
21	22	23	24	25	26	27
28	29	30				

OCTOBER						
S	M	T	W	T	F	S
			1	2	3	4
5	6	7	8	9	10	11
12	13	14	15	16	17	18
19	20	21	22	23	24	25
26	27	28	29	30	31	

NOVEMBER						
S	M	T	W	T	F	S
						1
2	3	4	5	6	7	8
9	10	11	12	13	14	15
16	17	18	19	20	21	22
23/30	24	25	26	27	28	29

DECEMBER						
S	M	T	W	T	F	S
	1	2	3	4	5	6
7	8	9	10	11	12	13
14	15	16	17	18	19	20
21	22	23	24	25	26	27
28	29	30				

HOLIDAYS

HOLIDAY	2013	2014	2015	2016
New Year's Day	January 1	January 1	January 1	January 1
Martin Luther King Jr. Day	January 21	January 20	January 19	January 18
Lincoln's Birthday	February 12	February 12	February 12	February 12
Valentine's Day	February 14	February 14	February 14	February 14
Presidents' Day	February 18	February 17	February 16	February 15
Ash Wednesday	February 13	March 5	February 18	February 10
Washington's Birthday	February 22	February 22	February 22	February 22
Daylight Saving Time Begins	March 10	March 9	March 8	March 13
Palm Sunday	March 24	April 13	March 29	March 20
Passover	March 26	April 15	April 4	April 23
Good Friday	March 29	April 18	April 3	March 25
Easter	March 31	April 20	April 5	March 27
Mother's Day	May 12	May 11	May 10	May 8
Memorial Day	May 27	May 26	May 25	May 30
Flag Day	June 14	June 14	June 14	June 14
Father's Day	June 16	June 15	June 21	June 19
Independence Day	July 4	July 4	July 4	July 4
Labor Day	September 2	September 1	September 7	September 5
Rosh Hashanah	September 5	September 25	September 14	October 3
Yom Kippur	September 14	October 4	September 23	October 12
Columbus Day	October 14	October 13	October 12	October 10
Daylight Saving Time Ends	November 3	November 2	November 1	November 6
Veterans Day	November 11	November 11	November 11	November 11
Thanksgiving	November 28	November 27	November 26	November 24
Hanukkah	November 28	December 17	December 7	December 25
Christmas	December 25	December 25	December 25	December 25

✧ ANNIVERSARY GIFTS ✧

	TRADITIONAL	MODERN
1st	Paper	Clocks
2nd	Cotton	China
3rd	Leather	Crystal, glass
4th	Linen (silk)	Appliances
5th	Wood	Silverware
6th	Iron	Wood objects
7th	Wool (copper)	Desk sets
8th	Bronze	Linens, lace
9th	Pottery (china)	Leather goods
10th	Tin, aluminum	Diamond
11th	Steel	Fashion jewelry
12th	Silk	Pearls, colored gems
13th	Lace	Textiles, furs
14th	Ivory	Gold jewelry
15th	Crystal	Watches
16th		Silver holloware
17th		Furniture
18th		Porcelain
19th		Bronze
20th	China	Platinum
21st		Brass, nickel
22nd		Copper
23rd		Silver plate
24th		Musical instruments
25th	Silver	Sterling silver
26th		Original pictures
27th		Sculpture
28th		Orchids
29th		New furniture
30th	Pearl	Diamond
31st		Timepieces
32nd		Conveyances (e.g., automobiles)
33rd		Amethyst
34th		Opal

	TRADITIONAL	MODERN
35th	Coral (jade)	Jade
36th		Bone china
37th		Alabaster
38th		Beryl, tourmaline
39th		Lace
40th	Ruby	Ruby
41st		Land
42nd		Improved real estate
43rd		Travel
44th		Groceries
45th	Sapphire	Sapphire
46th		Original poetry tribute
47th		Books
48th		Optical goods e.g., telescope, microscope
49th		Luxuries, any kind
50th	Gold	Gold
55th	Emerald	Emerald
60th	Diamond	Diamond
75th	Diamonds, diamondlike stones, gold	Diamonds, diamondlike stones, gold

❧ BIRTHSTONES & FLOWERS ❧

MONTHS	STONES	FLOWERS
January	Garnet	Carnation
February	Amethyst	Violet
March	Aquamarine	Daffodil
April	Diamond or White Topaz	Daisy
May	Emerald	Lily of the Valley
June	Pearl or Moonstone	Rose
July	Ruby	Larkspur
August	Peridot	Gladiolus
September	Sapphire	Aster
October	Opal	Calendula
November	Citrine	Chrysanthemum
December	Blue Topaz	Holly or Poinsettia

BIRTHDAYS

JANUARY

_____
_____
_____
_____
_____
_____
_____
_____
_____
_____
_____
_____
_____

FEBRUARY

_____
_____
_____
_____
_____
_____
_____
_____
_____
_____
_____
_____
_____

MARCH

_____
_____
_____
_____
_____
_____
_____
_____
_____
_____
_____
_____
_____

APRIL

_____
_____
_____
_____
_____
_____
_____
_____
_____
_____
_____

MAY

_____
_____
_____
_____
_____
_____
_____
_____
_____
_____
_____

JUNE

_____
_____
_____
_____
_____
_____
_____
_____
_____
_____
_____

JULY

AUGUST

SEPTEMBER

OCTOBER

NOVEMBER

DECEMBER

NAMES & NUMBERS

NAME	ADDRESS	TELEPHONE

NAME	ADDRESS	TELEPHONE

✎ A NOTE FROM THE EDITORS ✎

Guideposts Daily Planner 2012 is created each year by the Books and Inspirational Media Division of Guideposts, a nonprofit organization that touches millions of lives every day through products and services that inspire, encourage and uplift. Our magazines, books, prayer network (OurPrayer.org) and outreach programs help people connect their faith-filled values to daily life.

Your purchase of *Guideposts Daily Planner 2012* makes a difference. When you buy Guideposts products, you're helping fund our many outreach programs to military personnel, prisons, hospitals, nursing homes and educational institutions.

To learn more about our outreach ministry, visit GuidepostsFoundation.org. For more information about our other publications, such as *Daily Guideposts*, visit Guideposts.org or write Guideposts, PO Box 5815, Harlan, Iowa 51593.